WITCH ON ICE

WITCH ON ICE

BIGFOOT BAY WITCHES BOOK 1

CAT LARSON

Cover design by 100 Covers

THE BIGFOOT BAY WITCHES SERIES

Witch on Ice

Bewitched Brew

Witch Bane and The Croaking Game

Witch Haunt

The Witch is Back

The Big Day Brew-HaHa

CHAPTER ONE

*B*anana Jungle.

That was the name I'd just designated my 300-square-foot studio after nearly face-planting. Bridal mags cluttered the floor like peels, and I could barely take a step without slipping on a glossy. When you have a place the size of an ogre's shoebox, it doesn't take much to trash it up.

"Hoot! Hoot!" I even had a pack of wild animals housed next door. "Ooh eeh ah." Or a witch doctor. I banged on the paper-thin wall I shared with my neighbor to the left, not that it would do any good. I had no idea what they did in there, but I had to hear it at all hours of the day and night. "Squeak!"

I shook my head. Between the mess and the racket, I was living in pandemonium.

And I couldn't have been happier.

Because (drumroll, please)… Fernando proposed last night! An impromptu bending down on one knee in the park that had left me dumbstruck. Fortunately, it hadn't taken long to snap out of it and say yes. But once the screaming abated, I was thrown into a tizzy when I realized I hadn't the slightest clue how to

1

plan a wedding. Hence the magazines. We hit up a stand on the way home and wiped them clean of everything that had a white dress on the cover.

I glanced around the tiny space I'd been occupying for the past eight years. It was all mine and I loved it, but that didn't mean I wasn't ready for a change.

Fernando assured me that in no time at all we'd move into a nice big house, one with enough grass to require a lawn mower and enough land to anchor a swing set.

He said he had some money coming in soon, but for now, I was content. My place was home. It was normal. Blissfully normal. And at the moment, there was nothing more perfect than lying on my stomach on a freezing cold wood floor in the peak of Chicago winter, kicking up my heels and getting paper cuts while paging through wedding reception trends.

As I flipped over a corner, I stole a glimpse at my naked finger. So there wasn't a ring yet. No problem. There'd be one very soon. Along with the house, that was his promise. It'd all been so out of the blue. He told me it felt like the quintessential moment, and he couldn't wait a second longer to propose. So he didn't.

I thought it was romantic. Totally spontaneous, which was one of the qualities I loved about him so much. We'd only been together for a half a day over six months, and this was the last thing I was expecting, but when it was right, it was right, whether that be an hour or a decade. And since I was crazy about the guy, I decided to take a page from his playbook and be just as adventurous.

Meeting "The One," falling in love, getting engaged... that was how normal people lived their lives. They did run-of-the-mill things like buying a house, getting a dog or two, maybe having some kids, then spending their weekends camping or doing mundane chores like grocery shopping or scrubbing toilets.

Not frolicking under a full moon. Not uttering incantations over a bubbling potion. And especially not blowing up major appliances, terrifying the babysitter. The only magic I wanted to be associated with was the kind created when two hearts came together.

A thought wafted through my head, carrying with it an image of a boy I knew in school, but it was strewn aside by the here and now. Fernando. My *fiancé*.

I turned another page and... *squeal*. Wow. That dress. *The* dress. I was almost positive I not only wanted to walk down the aisle in it but also be buried in it, as well. Ugh. Gruesome. Abort that thought. I shut the magazine. It wasn't the style of the dress that mattered anyway. I could get married in a burlap sack and everything would still be stellar.

I checked the time. It was a hair over 7:00 p.m. in Peru, which also just happened to be local time as well. That sure made it convenient whenever I needed to get a hold of my parents. They'd be bunkering down soon for the night; it was call now or wait until morning. Either way, it'd be hit or miss. Their connection was shaky at best, and I couldn't always reach them anyway. If there was a true emergency, there were ways to get the word out, but I didn't think this constituted an emergency, even if it felt like an issue of top priority to me.

After all, their firstborn was engaged, and this was some big news. Huge. Monumental.

I picked up my cell and began punching in the number when mid-dial my sister's flaming hair popped on the screen.

My younger sister. My only sister. With her, I wasn't too thrilled to share the news since she'd be equally as thrilled to hear it.

I was about to ignore her in favor of speaking with someone

3

who would actually be happy for me when I reluctantly accepted the call. Might as well get it over with; she'd find out soon enough anyway.

"Hey, Violet—"

"You need to get here. *Now.*"

"What?" I bit the sides of my cheeks to contain the laughter. By "here," my overly dramatic sister meant Bigfoot Bay. Otherwise known as my freaky hometown almost two hours away. *Sure, Sis. I'll be right there.* "What crisis did you get yourself into this time? Did you—"

The sound of Fernando's voice stopped me cold. The floor beneath me suddenly felt like a warm beach.

"Samm... I'm so sorry..." There were words I couldn't decipher. Arguing in the background. Commotion. Fernando's angry tone caused me to leap up.

"Violet! What is going on? What's he doing there?"

She didn't respond. If it weren't for all the muffled ruckus, I would've thought she'd disconnected the call. I wasn't paying attention and skidded over a slick insert sprawled open on the floor, almost nosediving into my glass end table.

Argh. What *was* he doing there? They had no business even being in the same room together. It wasn't safe. Not with the way she felt about him. He was supposed to be here with me, not in another state with someone who despised him. We had dinner plans this evening. We were supposed to be discussing whatever it was that engaged couples discussed, for criminy's sake.

"Violet, answer me. I swear—"

The crashing of glass had me running for the door. At least it sounded like breaking glass, but with my sister involved, who knew? Son of a... Now, I was really worried. I made it out to the hallway when I realized I didn't have my purse or my car keys. Wouldn't get too far without them. Despite the wisdom of bumper stickers, my alternate form of transportation was not a broom.

Another loud bang sent me to the ceiling. It was like they were hosting a cymbal convention. Their voices rose higher, but still, I couldn't make out anything besides a few expletives. I went back and snatched my purse, then darted out to the street, taking the steps two at a time. I dropped the call. If she wasn't going to answer me, I had to try someone who would.

I multitasked, ringing up my fiancé while sprinting across the parking lot and praying that cars would stay out of my path. What good would I do anyone if I were flattened to the asphalt?

Pick up, pick up, pick up, I silently pleaded as I hopped in my car.

"Eve."

I let out a huge puff of air that quickly formed into a misty cloud. It was blasted cold out here. I started up the ignition which I knew would need several minutes before it was even ready to drive.

"Fernando, thank goodness. Please tell me—"

A lightning bolt struck me dumb, causing my eardrum to sizzle. What the...? It wasn't even storming out. I yanked my cell away, expecting to see smoke billowing from it. I could certainly smell it. My hand and entire ear felt like they were on fire, but when I rubbed my other hand against them, they were just slightly warm.

An explosion of fear burst through me. "Fernando!" I screamed.

No answer. I couldn't even get a signal. My battery had been full just a moment before, but now it'd been zapped dead. I let out another shriek. I had no charger in the car and couldn't waste time going back inside to get one. I tossed the phone aside and immediately went into autopilot, forcing my poor cold engine to move before its time like I was kicking an exhausted horse to gallop faster.

Conscious thought had not returned until I was crossing the border into Wisconsin, convinced that a tribe of amphetamine-loving flying monkeys was carrying me. I had no idea how I'd made it so quickly, thanking my lucky stars that we weren't in the middle of a nasty blizzard.

I tried to make sense of everything I knew so far, tried packaging it up into a nice sparkly box of understanding.

The best I got was a dented-up tackle box with lots of jagged, sharp hooks inside.

The only thing I knew for certain was that my man possessed a kind heart. He knew that my sister and I didn't see eye to eye on some things (okay, most things). After he'd proposed, he was curious who I'd pick to be my maid of honor. He didn't come right out and say it, but I was sure he was hinting at Violet. I told him straight out that I'd never ask her, and even if I did, she'd never accept. As far as he knew, we had a falling-out when we were kids and never fully reconciled. End of story.

Because really, what was I supposed to say? I could just imagine that conversation: *Hey, sweetie, guess what? Your future wife is a witch—a recovering one, so no problem there—but oh, by the way, the rest of the family has a completely different outlook. You see, they're full-blown witches and proud of it. What? Witches aren't real, you say? Ha! You're in for a rude awakening then, my love. And did I forget to mention one teensy-weensy detail? My magical genes are dominant and can be passed down to any offspring.*

But don't worry. I've been doing just fine all these years suppressing my witchy side. It won't even be an issue. Barely. No, really, I'm perfectly sane. Honest.

What's that, honey? You're not sure you can handle this right now and need some time to think about it?

Ugh. I gave my head a sharp shake, forcing myself back to the present. Good thing too, considering I was operating heavy machinery at seventy miles per hour.

Nope, not a conversation I'd be eager to have any time soon, if ever. I was not a fan of keeping secrets, but this was the type of destructive skeleton that could come out and rip your head clean off. I liked Fernando's head right where it was, thank you very much.

I gripped the steering wheel and plowed forward, passing a sign stating the Bigfoot Bay exit was only ten miles away. If I'd remembered correctly, after I turned off the freeway, it'd be at least fifteen minutes of rural driving if I kept to the speed limit. I pushed the pedal down to eighty.

I couldn't stop freaking out about those two in the same vicinity. My fiancé's spontaneity had likely caused him to rush over and speak with my sister, probably hoping to convince her to make amends with me in time for our wedding. Sweet guy.

On the other side of the coin, Violet was a troll in a china shop. What was even worse than having a reckless sister with a rash temper was a reckless sister with a rash temper who also happened to detest human males. *"It's just as easy to fall in love with a magical man than a weak one."* She'd want no part of being a sister-in-law to a lowly man, and I had no idea what she might do if she discovered that would be the case. Fernando may be the epitome of strength in the human world—there were bulls named after him, for Pete's sake—but next to my sister he might as well have all the power of an ant underneath someone's shoe.

I stole a glance at my phone, and my insides twisted. For all I knew she had already fried him up like a common piece of bacon.

At least my brain had finally stopped buzzing, no longer feeling like a bag of burnt microwave popcorn. That clarity allowed me to talk myself out of taking the country roads at a wild pace, endangering all the cows that might have wandered out for a late-night snack.

At least the streets were devoid of traffic. Even on the freeway, the other drivers had steered clear of me. It was as if they sensed a psychotic bride-to-be behind the wheel.

When the speed limit dropped to twenty-five, my chest was pounding so hard it was going to leap through my skull. With all the adrenaline coursing through me, I could've run faster than this. I clenched my jaw and crept on, crawling into Bigfoot Bay.

Once I crossed over into the small lake town, everything seemed to change. I was no longer surrounded by acres of barns and farmland but storybook cottages and lush forests. Despite my unfortunate experiences here, I couldn't deny it was one of the most beautiful places in the world. Too bad it was also one of the wackiest.

I drove directly to my sister's shop, Violet's Soap & Tea Emporium. It wasn't until I was swinging into a parking spot when I took a quick second to consider how I'd arrived so effortlessly. I'd left the town when I was below driving age, yet I knew exactly where I was going. Not only that, Violet only had her shop for a couple of years and I'd only seen it in pictures. Huh. The flying monkeys must've doubled as a navigation device.

I rolled my eyes. *That's quite enough, Eve.* Of course, I knew how to get around. Downtown Bigfoot Bay was designed like every other downtown small town in America. I got lucky, is all.

I jumped out of the car and darted up to the door. I had a raging case of nerves that only intensified as I neared the unlit shop. In fact, the entire street was dark and deserted, considering the hour of day and time of year. If it weren't for the moon, I wouldn't have even seen my feet in front of me.

Snowflakes picked that moment to fall, powdering my face as I rattled the locked door. "Violet!" I pounded and yelled, then reeled it in, remembering where I was. Even though it appeared no one was around, it wasn't wise to make a scene. I'd have to do all my screaming mentally. My sister had converted part of her store into a living space, and it was likely that there were other shop owners who'd done the same. I couldn't afford to have someone report me for attempted breaking and entering.

I took a calming breath and peered inside. Not one light was on. I pressed my ear to the frosty window as if expecting to hear something. Anything. By all accounts, it appeared the place was empty. The gnawing sensation eating its way through my gut would not ease up. It was too quiet around here. Eerily quiet. Or maybe I was just used to the nonstop hustle and bustle of the city. Either way, it unnerved me to no end.

A shrill ring nearly did me in. I vaulted back, slipping on the slick concrete and landing smack on the cold wet ground. I picked myself up and dusted off. I guess it could've been much worse.

It was then I noticed Fernando's car wasn't there. The absence of it hadn't even registered when I'd first arrived, being in such a tizzy and all. I scanned the street as flakes turned into cubes, pelting into my eyes. An unexpected snowstorm seemed to materialize out of nowhere, but at least it had waited until I arrived.

My vision was limited, but from what I could see, his car was not nearby. Unless he'd parked far down the block, he was gone. That was good, right? It meant I could finally relax again. I chuckled. We had probably unknowingly passed each other on the freeway.

So then why did my stomach still feel like I'd swallowed rusty razor blades?

The ringing resumed, startling me once again. It took a moment before I realized what it was and where it was coming from. It was my phone, my jacket pocket. The same phone that had been dead not too long before, lying on my car seat.

When did I put it in my pocket?

I pulled it out carefully as if it had teeth, noticing that the battery was now at a hundred percent. Okay, this was just plain ludicrous, and I had no time for it. I needed to get back home to Fernando. I was shivering, I was starving, and I was spent. Worst of all, it appeared I'd overreacted just a tad, and now I had to drive home in a blizzard.

After staring a while at my ringing cell, I hit Accept. It was my mom, after all. Or at least that was what my screen read. It could have been an impersonating spirit who'd charged up my battery. No, wait… I had that backward. Ghosts drained energy from devices, not replenished them.

"Hi, Mom. Can I call you back later? This isn't the best—"

"Samm." My mom sighed. "Am I glad I got a hold of you."

"Remember it's… never mind. What's up?" I'd been going by Eve, my middle name, since I left Bigfoot Bay thirteen years prior, but did that make any difference to my mom? Nope. No matter how many times I told her to call me Eve, she ignored me. "How's Dad?"

"Your father's fine. He sends his love. But I've been trying to reach your sister with no luck. I've had the strangest feeling for the past several hours, and it's only gotten worse. When was the last time you spoke with her?"

I walked back to my car. The sooner we got off the phone, the sooner I could try calling Fernando.

"Well—"

"You have to check on her."

"What? Why?"

"I already told you."

"Right. Your strange feeling." *Get in line, Mom.* I huffed then watched as a cloud of air danced in front of me. The temperature felt like it'd dropped another ten degrees, turning me into a walking ice woman. "It just so happens that I'm at her place and she's not home."

"You're... you're in Bigfoot Bay?" The utter disbelief in her voice wasn't the least bit surprising. I hadn't stepped foot here again after I'd left. "So, you felt it too—about Violet?"

I got in my car and cranked on the heat. "Not exactly."

"You have to check on her," she repeated.

"I told you she's not home. And now I'm going home. I'll try reaching her later." She could be sure of that. Violet wasn't off the hook. Not by a long shot. She had plenty of explaining to do and so did Fernando. Once I was certain of his safety, I was going to wring his neck for putting himself in jeopardy, even if he wasn't aware that's what he was doing.

"Samm?"

Now, I just had to think of a logical reason why he couldn't be around Violet anymore. Something along the lines of my sister was criminally insane and had an ax to grind with men. Literally.

"Samm!"

"What?"

"Aren't you listening to me? I've been talking to you."

"Sorry." I turned on the windshield wipers, but it didn't seem to do much good. The glass blanketed white again the moment the blades cleared. Great. It was going to be a fun drive.

"I don't care if you say she's not home. You're there for a reason, and I'd sleep much better tonight knowing you went inside and looked around."

"The door's locked."

"There's a key underneath the flowerpot."

Of course, there was. The only spot more obvious would be under the welcome mat. It was Bigfoot Bay, after all. People here were more likely to scrub a dirty window for you than to break into one.

I dropped my head. "Fine," I grumbled, turning off my car and grabbing my purse. "I'll call you back when—"

"You'll do no such thing. I'm going to stay on with you."

"Fine."

The line crackled as I headed up the snow-covered path. I didn't know how long before we'd be disconnected anyway. I was amazed it was holding out this long. The service on her archaic flip phone in her remote little village was more miss than hit.

I trudged up to the front entrance again and felt around with my foot for the flowerpot. If Mother Nature didn't let up soon, we'd be under a state of emergency.

"Are you inside yet?"

"Mom, I'm still looking for the key. Everything's buried here. Not everyone is basking in a tropical paradise."

I kicked over the pot then rooted around for the frozen key with my equally frozen fingers. *Ah, gotcha.*

"It's almost ten. Why isn't she home?"

I paused with the key halfway to the lock. Good question. Where the heck *was* she? Violet didn't own a car, preferring to walk everywhere. It hadn't even occurred to me until then that she could've left somewhere with Fernando. Was it against his will? I quickly booted that distressing possibility from my mind lest I freak out again.

"You know, she could just be sleeping," I said, for as much as my assurance as my mother's.

"No, she would've woken up and answered my call."

"The weather's bad. Maybe there's a line down somewhere."

Another thing my sister didn't own—a cell phone. She refused, claiming they scrambled her energy. So, a downed phone line was a plausible reason for her not answering, but I failed to mention that the snow hadn't started until after I'd arrived.

I keyed open the door and stepped inside. "Violet!" I yelled. "Violet, I know you're hiding. Come out and—" *Pfff.* A head of lettuce assaulted me. What in the world? I blew it aside, tasting the bitterness on my lips. Not lettuce.

"What's happening?"

"I just got a faceful of something leafy and bitter." I wiped my mouth with the back of my hand. Blech. Maybe it was her equivalent of a security system. I hoped it wasn't poisonous.

"That's mugwort," my mother said. "A protective herb. You'd know that if—"

"All right, all right." I didn't need a lecture. "Violet?" I felt along the wall for a light switch.

"What do you see?"

"I don't see anything. I can't find a light." I jabbed my hipbone into something sharp. *Dang it!* It was throbbing now. My eyes were taking too long to acclimate to the darkness, and unless I found a switch soon, I'd end up black and blue.

"Forget about that. What do you sense?"

"I don't sense anything either. Look, she's not here, okay? I'm sure everything's fine. Maybe your bad feeling was just some undercooked river fish."

"Sammara Eve Hain. Do not take that tone with me. You know better."

I sighed. She was pulling out the big guns. "Just Eve is fine, you know."

It'd fall on deaf ears, of course, but it couldn't hurt to keep trying. Just like she did. There'd been some pretty high hopes for me, after all, being the firstborn female in the family. I mean, come on… I'm named Sammara, shortened to Samm.

Samm *Hain*. As in Samhain, Celtic for summer's end. Just toss my middle name at the end and you've got Samhain Eve.

Otherwise known as Halloween.

Hilarious, right?

Yeah, I was aware it wasn't pronounced the same as the actual Gaelic word, but tomayto, tomahto. When it was written down, the matter became moot anyway. Either my mother had indulged in too much dandelion wine right before filling out my birth certificate or she'd been that desperate to secure my witchy future by choosing a symbolic namesake. Seeing as I had never noticed her touch a drop of anything harder than iced tea, all bets go to the latter.

Meanwhile, my sister, Violet Rose, got the pretty flowery name. And what happened? She ended up being the one who embraced her witchery with all the grace of a pack of rabid wildebeests.

"Sammara Eve Hain, are you listening to me?"

"Yes, Mom." Had she been talking?

"Just because you turned your back on your gifts doesn't mean you can insult those who didn't. I know exactly what I felt, and it wasn't bad fish."

"Yes, Mom." I tried not to snort at "gifts." "Sorry."

In our family, we were blessed (cursed) with magical talents that came to us naturally. One so-called practical divination skill was uncloaked at birth and heavily nurtured right out of the womb. The rest could be mastered with lots of study and practice. And even then, it wasn't guaranteed unless you were born with it.

My inborn skill was fire reading. Seriously? How practical was that? In a nutshell, it was candle-gazing. I would've been better prepared for life learning how to clean out a chimney or knit a scarf. The frustration that arose from my useless teaching only proved I wasn't meant to follow my witchy path, and it hadn't hurt me in the least to shun it all these years. On the contrary. I was much better off pretending to be a normal human female.

"Turn a blind eye to it all you want, Samm. It's still a part of you."

The connection crackled again, and I hoped this would be the time I lost her. No such luck. I twirled a piece of hair around my finger as the room finally began to come into focus. I couldn't discern everything, but so far, nothing appeared broken or out of place, certainly nothing like I had imagined when I'd heard those crashes.

"Violet?" I called once more while crossing the room, still in search of light.

"I'm not sure how long my service will hold out. I want your promise right now that you'll stay there however long it takes until you're sure your sister's safe and sound."

"What? No. I can't do that. I have a life, a job." *A fiancé.* "I can't just camp out here."

At last. I spotted a small stained-glass lamp in the corner, and I went over and tugged the cord. The bulb was dim, but it'd do.

"Oh really? And what's the job-of-the-month this time?"

"Not fair, Mom." I wasn't about to tell her I was actually in between jobs. Again. "Just because I haven't discovered my passion yet like Violet..." My eyes raked over dozens of little jars, lining the built-in shelves. Since tea was part of her store name, I assumed they were filled with tea leaves, but for all I knew, they contained ground-up toad warts and graveyard dust.

"And you know exactly why that is, don't you?"

"Um, maybe because I haven't found anything that resonates with me yet? I'm still young. I have plenty of time to decide the rest of my life."

I turned around, spying bars of soap interspersed among

boxes of stationery. Lots of stationery. Who wrote letters by hand anymore? My baby sister was more old-fashioned than my parents.

If Violet was playing hide-and-seek, there were only a couple more places to check—the "Employees Only" room that looked nothing more than an herb-infested supply closet (I peeked) and a backroom leading to what had to be her living quarters.

My mom snickered. "And nothing will ever satisfy you, dear daughter, until you wake up and follow your—"

"All right. I'll stay, okay?"

Geez. She acted like my desire to lead an ordinary life was just a phase I'd eventually grow out of, like the terrible twos. At least my father was more sympathetic, seeing as his magic was dormant. Anything dealt to my sister and me at birth was all courtesy of the maternal bloodline.

"Thank you, Samm. Now, that wasn't so hard, was it?" I grunted. "You know I worry about you girls. I didn't want to mention this at first, but I heard it the other day." She whispered, "Did you?"

"Do you mean static? Because I'm hearing plenty of that right now." We'd probably lose connection at any moment. I pushed open the door to the backroom, seeing an unmade bed. I stepped inside.

"Don't change the subject. You know very well what I meant. The—"

The call dropped, along with the battery life, and I ignored the heebie-jeebies swirling in my stomach. I would not let her superstitious nature infect me. Besides, for all I knew, she'd heard the cry of a howler monkey, not "The Shriek." The screaming omen was already taken seriously enough in our family; I didn't need to encourage her further.

Torrential nausea bubbled inside me, and I stuffed that

down too. My mom was being ridiculous. It was just some wild animal; I was sure of it. She was in the middle of a rainforest, after all. I massaged my midsection briskly as my eyes caught sight of a scattering of grass on the floor.

Grass?

The low-wattage bulbs in the place weren't doing my vision any favors, so I crouched down to get a better look. I picked up a blade and rubbed it between my fingers. It certainly felt like grass, but the kind found in the peak of spring, not the brown, lifeless stuff that was currently lying dormant under the snow outside.

I squinted, taking in the rest of the surrounding scene. There was an object a little farther ahead, so I moved in closer. It looked like... My insides churned violently; I couldn't tame it any longer. On the hardwood floor of my sister's bedroom lay a charred cell phone—*Fernando's* cell phone—and right beside it sat a large frog. The blood rushed from my head at an alarming pace.

He croaked.

I passed out.

CHAPTER TWO

I woke a short time later to something cool on my throat. I peeked open an eye and rubbed the back of my head, more confused than a leprechaun in a Skittles factory. What the heck was going on, and why was I on the ground? Why did it feel like I'd been clobbered by a two-by-four? And why was there a...

"Ahhhh!" I leaped up and the 'something cool' was flung to the side. It took a moment to get my bearings in order to comprehend what that something was. Or rather someone.

Oh no, oh no, oh no.

I scooped him up and cradled him in my palms. "I'm sorry. I'm so, so sorry." His bulging eyes blinked up at me. "You're not hurt, are you?"

Croak.

Holy crud. Of course, he couldn't answer me. Not in a language I understood. I had to lie down again. My legs wobbled, my head ached, and my formerly large, muscled fiancé was small enough to fit in my hand. Not to mention also soft and squishy like a water balloon. Wanting to cry was an understatement.

"Violet!" I howled. "You are not getting away with this!"

I couldn't break down. Not yet. I had to keep it together. I set Fernando on the floor gently, and he hopped away. He didn't appear physically harmed from my tossing him aside earlier, but I swore he looked a little insulted over my reaction. Not that I knew the first thing about what a frog looked like when its feelings were hurt.

I dropped my head in my hands. Jiminy Cricket… I had to find Violet. *Now.* She would pay for this big-time. I sidled over and stroked his smooth back. He wouldn't even blink at me this time. With either eyelid. Great. I'd emotionally wounded my amphibian fiancé.

"You are not getting away with this, Violet!" I reiterated loudly as if my underhanded sister were lurking in the shadows. "You hear me? You've gone too far this time."

This was worse than everything else she'd ever done put together. Worse than the time she had used a spell to warm up her hot chocolate, starting the curtains on fire and blaming it on me. Worse than the time she'd turned my goldfish into a miniature dragon because she thought it was a cooler pet. Even worse than the time she'd attempted to bring her favorite doll to life, ending up changing our babysitter into a plastic figurine instead. Talk about a total quagmire, at least until Mom came along and straightened it out.

And believe me, there was more. *Much* more. But at least all those times could've been chalked up to her youth and immaturity. Now, she knew better. Juvenility was not a cute trait in a twenty-three-year-old.

I muttered under my breath. She just couldn't accept my being in love with a human, could she? It wasn't enough that she couldn't stand men. No. She had to control how I ran my life too. Argh. I was going to blow a gasket.

After pacing around the shop for a while in a futile attempt to cool down, I picked up the stupid landline phone only to discover it was still as dead as Caesar's ghost. I needed to get a hold of my mom again, although she wouldn't be able to fix Violet's mess this time. Now that she'd entered adulthood, she was the only one who could reverse the spell. And she was nowhere in sight.

Goodbye nice, normal life. Hello... *Stop it, Eve. Pull yourself together for Fernando's sake.*

I took a deep breath, then opened the front door to an icy blast that almost knocked me backward. I quickly shut it, scanning the floor in a panic. I felt a rush of relief when I saw Fernando in the corner. I had to be more careful opening up doors now. If he had leaped out, I could have lost him forever.

I stared out the window at the whiteout conditions. It was as if the town had been buried in several feet of snow. I couldn't even see my car parked on the street. Despite that, I had to brave the weather and find Fernando's car, now that I was convinced Violet had taken off in it. Just because she preferred to walk didn't mean she didn't know how to drive.

Well, if she thought she would hide away for a few hours, coming back when the coast was clear, she was out of her freaking mind. I was not going *anywhere* until my fiancé was walking on two legs again.

My phone hadn't magically recharged again and sitting around wouldn't accomplish a thing. I stormed into Violet's bedroom and grabbed a pair of boots from her closet, along with a hat. Movement in the corner of my eye showed that I hadn't entered alone. Putting on my best smile, I bent down and touched his little head.

On a whim, I closed my eyes and kissed him. Hey, it always worked in fairy tales. I slowly lifted a lid.

Croak.

I sighed. Fairy tales were frauds.

"It's going to be okay. I promise. I'll get us out of this one way or another."

Finding my sister was the first step to his freedom, and time was of the essence. I slipped out, closing the door behind me and sheltering him inside the bedroom. I couldn't have him springing all over the place while I was gone and risk him getting into her crazy concoctions. When his safety was assured, I grabbed the key that'd been stowed under the flowerless flowerpot and locked the shop on my way out. It was foolish to drive so I was forced to come up with plan B.

Icy thick flakes whipped into me as I slogged down the street or sidewalk or brittle winter grass. At this point, I hadn't a clue what I was stepping on. I kept my head down, beginning to feel like I was the last one alive. It was trance-like. It took the flashing light of a plow to bring me back to reality.

Fortunately, another light also beaconed in the distance. The Bigfoot Bay police station. Just the place I was looking for. I changed course and pushed my feet through the unshoveled walk. When I finally entered the building, the fresh-faced officer manning the front desk jumped up.

"Miss?" He rushed over. "Are you hurt? Was there an accident?"

At least I was still identifiable; I hadn't been mistaken for a yeti. I shook myself off, layers of snow tumbling to the floor.

"No, I'm fine." Physically. I stomped my boots, hoping to thaw out my toes. "Sorry about that." I'd just made one heck of a slushy mess for someone. I glanced around. He appeared to be the only one in the small station. "If you point me toward a mop I can—"

"Never mind that. What in tarnation are you doing out in this weather at this hour? I sure hope you're not driving."

I stifled a giggle. He reminded me of a sweet cop from the early '60s. Living in Chicago for half my life, it was easy to forget that towns like this still existed. Ones where the biggest crime committed was garden gnome theft.

"Nope. I walked here." I would've thought that'd been obvious by the white blanket dripping off of me. "Is Officer Kane around by chance?"

"No, he's out. Can I help you with something?"

He handed me a cup of hot coffee, and I accepted it graciously. It was weak and stale, but it tasted better than anything I could've imagined at the moment.

"Um…" I wasn't sure. For this matter, I really wanted to speak with someone familiar. "I don't know."

"Miss, if you need help, you know it's my job to assist you."

Right. To serve and protect. I thought of poor little Fernando the Frog and my blood boiled.

"Do you know Violet Hain?" He nodded. Stupid question. Of course, he did. Everyone knew everyone here. "I'm in town… visiting her. I'm her sister and—"

"Samm?"

"Actually, I go by Eve now."

"Wow, I cannot believe I didn't recognize you right away."

I studied his baby face, the overextended smile that only made his cheeks plumper. Cute kid. And much too young to be a cop. But who knew? Maybe he was just really well-rested.

"I'm sorry. Do I know you?"

"Mike. Mike Hansen. I was a year below you." He grinned. "You know, I had a bit of a crush on you back in the day." Okay, well this was awkward. I didn't recognize the face or the name. And how was I supposed to respond to his little confession? Thank you? "Wow, so you're back now. For how long?"

"Not sure. Um…" I really wished Officer Kane was here. "Are you able to find a car for me?"

"You need a car?"

"I don't need a car. I'm trying to locate one."

"Was it stolen?"

I tapped my chin, considering my answer. Stolen was accurate, but I didn't want to get Violet in trouble before I had a chance to kill her.

"More like misplaced. It's my boyfriend's car, rather my fiancé's." Mike glanced at my left hand wrapped around the Styrofoam cup, no doubt noticing my ringless finger. "I need to know where it is, and I thought maybe…" Maybe what? Maybe this was a dumb idea? Yeah, probably, but I'd been desperate.

"Ah, I see. You'll want a private investigator for that, um, issue. I can recommend one if you'd like."

I coughed up a sip of coffee then set down the cup. "It's nothing like that. You know what? It was silly of me to take up your time with such a *non*-issue. I'll just be going now."

I didn't need him thinking Fernando was off cheating on me and that was why I needed to know where his car was. And based on his raised eyebrows, that was exactly what he was thinking.

He gave me a funny look. Not that I blamed him. Who wanders out on a night like this, barging into a cop shop and making absurd requests?

"I can't leave the station, but I can call for a car to take you back. I'm assuming you're staying with Violet?" He picked up the receiver.

"No, please. That's not necessary. The walk isn't too far, and it's… refreshing. Thanks anyway."

His forehead creased further. "You sure about that?"

"Yep."

I headed for the door. "Okay, then. I'll be sure to tell Damon you stopped by."

I swiveled my head. "Damon?"

"Officer Kane. You did ask for him." Now, he looked downright alarmed. "Samm, are you sure you're okay?"

I chuckled. "It's Eve, remember? And I'm perfectly fine. I was asking for Jack Kane."

"Oh, I forget how long you've been gone. Jack is retired, traveling the world with the missus. I thought you were asking for his son."

I nodded. Of course. Damon had always talked about going into the academy and following in his father's footsteps. "No worries, then." I waved. "See you later."

"You be careful out there."

"Always."

I exited, confronting the blustery air once again. "Don't be a stranger now," Mike called out as the snow swirled around me in a whirlwind. I began the trek back to Violet's. Shoot. I should've asked Mike if he had a phone charger to borrow.

The walk back was easier than the walk there since I had a better sense of direction. When I arrived at her place, I shook off all the icy clumps and went inside, beelining directly to the bedroom. I experienced a slight anxiety attack imagining the toilet lid up with Fernando bobbing inside. There was a tiny bathroom connected to the bedroom. Had I remembered to close that door too?

All these little precautions that I would have never thought twice about before were worrying me sick now. I didn't know the first thing about caring for a frog. For his protection, I should've considered buying a tank, but I could not humiliate him like that.

Relief flooded through me when I noticed that the bathroom door was shut tight. I quickly scanned the floor, but he was nowhere to be found. I held myself back from rushing frantically around. That was how accidental squashings happened. Ugh.

"Fernando?" Could he understand me with his froggy eardrums? Could the cold-blooded recognize their name like a dog?

This was so, so wrong.

"Fernando!" I checked all over the bedroom, in the corners, in every nook and cranny. Even under the bed. I was baffled. The room was barely larger than a galley kitchen, for heaven's sake.

I plopped down on the bed, almost accomplishing what I'd been terrified to do with my foot. Oh no... I almost sat on the poor guy. Wait, what? I peered closer. No wonder I hadn't seen him. He'd taken on a silver shade to blend in with the comforter. I picked him up and he immediately began to change back. Huh. I guess enchanted animals followed a different set of rules because I was pretty sure your everyday green frog didn't act like a chameleon. Maybe it meant he could understand me, after all.

As he cuddled in my lap, I was overcome with emotion. Tears gathered below my lids, and it didn't take long before a fat drop rolled down my cheek. I just wanted my old life back. I wanted my man to hold *me*.

"You're not getting out of this much longer, you know," I said with a weak laugh, wiping my wet face with the back of my hand. "I'm going to get that ring on my finger. You hear me?"

He made a noise between a chirp and a bark, and I took that as an affirmative. A second later, the room filled with a high-pitched ringing sound that startled me enough to nearly send him flying again. Geez. Even I was a danger to him. How would he ever get through this ordeal in one piece?

Wait a leaping moment. My phone. It was my phone

ringing. My *dead* phone. I set Fernando down on the blanket and dashed out. What had charged it this time?

The screen displayed an unknown number and a fully charged battery. I was almost scared to answer, but it could be Violet.

"Hello?"

"Yeah, hi. I'd like to order a large pepperoni."

"What?"

"Isn't this Sasquatch Pizza?"

"No, it's not."

Click. I pulled the phone away with a frown. Then I watched as it quickly drained back down to zero. Argh. I tossed it across the room, and it skittered into the wall.

Just what I needed on top of everything else—a haunted cell phone.

I returned to the bedroom and resumed my position on the bed. Fernando hopped onto my stomach. If anything, we were going to have a memorable story for the grandkids. There'd be no hiding my witchy family now.

There was only one question left after all was said and done.

Would he forgive me?

CHAPTER THREE

When the morning light rolled around, I was exhausted, barely having slept more than a dozen minutes at a time. Fernando hadn't budged from my stomach, curling up in the folds of my warm sweater. Did frogs curl up?

I sat up and held my head in my hands. Oh man... it was not all some bad dream. I took a few minutes to stare down at him while he slept. He was currently sporting a lovely shade of turquoise. My stomach roared loudly, waking him, and he jumped off.

I touched his back. "I'm sorry. Did I scare you?" This was so, so wrong. I had the feeling I'd be saying that a whole heck of a lot before this was all over. And it would be soon, I swore. It was a brand new day, and I was going to set this right. Somehow.

But first, I needed to fill my stomach. When was the last time Fernando had eaten? He was probably starving as well. I was responsible for making sure he ate now too. Oh man, what if he'd only eat centipedes and horseflies? Ick.

Quit being such a baby, Eve. I stood and put on my big-girl pants. If he had to endure living in a little amphibian body, then I could easily deal with some bugs.

I used a spare toothbrush I found under the sink, then took the quickest shower in the history of showers, coming out feeling dirtier than when I went in. But that was okay. I couldn't waste time on such things this morning. I didn't even wash my hair, just threw it back in a ponytail. Violet's clothes would have to suffice since I hadn't exactly thought to pack an overnight bag when I ran out the door the night before.

After throwing on one of her sweaters and a pair of jeans, I patted Fernando on the head. "Before you know it, you'll be back to your handsome self." I was going to be all unicorns and rainbows today. I'd force myself because the alternative was going stark raving mad. I had to be the rock for both of us. "Not saying you're not handsome now, of course, but, um… never mind." Ugh. Hopefully, I hadn't offended him again.

I peeked out the bedroom door to see sunlight streaming through the windows. I went over, noticing that all the streets had been plowed and there was actual life outside. Not a lot because the town still had a couple of months until tourist season started, but there were a good handful of locals out and about. I wasn't sure when the blizzard had finally let up, but the snow was now all piled up nice and neat, disguising its hazardous side. If I were still a kid, I would've been rushing out to sled and build forts.

My eyelids drooped, hitting me with just how tired I was, and the day had barely started. If I was going to get through it with half a mind, I needed coffee *stat*. Unfortunately, a search of the shop hadn't turned up a single bean. Only nasty, musty leaves. Otherwise known as tea. Blech.

But I did find a loaf of chocolate chip bread in the mini-fridge. Three loaves, to be exact, all wrapped up tightly, one missing a tiny bite. I peeled back the plastic wrap on the bitten one and sniffed. Banana. Darn. I would've devoured it if it were just plain chocolate, but banana made me queasy. My growling stomach urged me to reconsider and suffer the consequences, but I quickly shoved it back into the fridge before I could regret it.

After more rooting around, I found a couple oat bars that looked suspiciously healthy, but at least they contained chocolate. I broke off a piece and discovered that it was just its imposter, carob. Oh well, good enough. I declared it edible and scarfed it down while mentally listing out the day's agenda in order of importance: coffee, pet store, Fernando's car. *Gah!* Violet could be all the way to Canada by now. Although, her entire life was here. I couldn't imagine her leaving it for too long. She couldn't stay away forever. I glanced through the slightly open bedroom door and stopped shoveling food into my pie hole in case Fernando was watching.

Feeling guilty, I offered him a piece but he didn't bite. Then I yanked it away. What if carob was toxic to frogs like chocolate was to dogs? Just because he was bewitched, didn't mean he had a completely different physiology than a regular frog. Or did it? Maybe he didn't have to eat at all and just magically survived on air. No, that was one theory I would not be testing out. I wasn't about to starve my poor fiancé before I could even get him human again. I hung my head. There was so much I had to learn.

I snapped it back up with a large smile. Nope. Miss Positivity, remember? "Don't worry, sweetie. We'll find you something you like." Even if that something happened to be crawling and wriggling. I'd hand-feed him if I had to.

Before I left, I checked my phone that I'd tossed into the corner. Maybe I'd knocked some sense into it. I expected to see a cracked screen, but it was still intact. Albeit still dead. Another thing to add to my to-do list: Pick up a charger for my haunted cell.

For the heck of it, I tried Violet's landline and got a dial tone. That was a good sign. The storm had likely messed with the wires and now everything was good to go. I dialed up my mom but had no luck getting through. I'd try again later. Oh, she was going to hear about this. No doubt about that.

I made a note to call Mrs. Geller when I returned to ask her to keep an eye on my place. My elderly Chicago neighbor was the only approachable one in the building. Everyone else was either too busy or preferred to keep to themselves. Fortunately, she lived in the unit right across from me and was a natural-born busybody who'd befriended me. She'd let me know if she saw anything suspicious. Who knew when I'd be back again? I could be evicted first.

As long as I had Fernando the Man back nothing else mattered. I could move in with him if needed. I pulled on my coat and was halfway out the door when I paused. It didn't feel right leaving him alone again, especially when I had no idea how long this would take. I stepped outside and gauged the temperature. The sun was warm on my face, lessening the chill, but it was probably only about thirty degrees. Was that too cold for an enchanted frog?

I dumped out the entire contents of my purse, save for some cash that I zippered up in a side pocket, and stuffed a couple of Violet's scarves inside. Then I placed Fernando in the makeshift bed. There, all soft and cozy. I almost hoped he'd poop all over them. It'd serve her right.

I'd just have to take him with me wherever I went. I was planning to drive, but one look at my snow-crusted car and I decided to hoof it. It'd take way too long to scrape, and I didn't want to waste precious time. Everything I needed was within a few blocks anyway. Almost everything. In the time that both of us were fed, there was a good chance the sun would take care of most of the clean-up, and I could spend the rest of the day searching for Violet.

As I ventured down the street, I was in awe over how much hadn't changed—and how much I still remembered. It was like I'd never left. I could recall each store, each crack in the sidewalk as if it were yesterday. I wasn't sure how that made me feel since I'd never intended to ever come back.

There was the candy shoppe/ice cream parlor on the right. The upscale boutique to my left. The multitude of gift shops that were closed for the season but would soon be bustling all summer long. The family-style restaurant that served the best gingerbread pancakes, and ooh... just a street over near the waterfront was Caliente—the best Mexican food on the planet. My stomach rumbled something fierce.

I quickened my pace. On the corner up ahead was Murphy's Pet Store. And *score!* There appeared to be a coffee house right next door, replacing what I thought had been a puzzle outlet.

I popped into Bigfoot Café first for a quick to-go cup of the darkest brew they made. The kid behind the counter looked like she should've been behind a desk instead. At Bigfoot Bay Middle School. She eyed me with all the curiosity reserved for an outsider, and I supposed I was. I'd been gone for over a decade. But just like that, her expression changed.

"Anything else?" she asked, handing me the steaming cup. I shook my head and plunked on a lid. "Do I know you?"

"I don't think so. I'm just visiting." I glanced over at the food case. "On second thought, can I take one of those ham and egg sandwiches?" Maybe Fernando would share it with me, and I could get away with skipping the pet store.

"Sure." The barista placed one in the warmer. "You here for the festival this weekend?"

Festival? "No."

"Seems a strange time to visit, then. Most people aren't here in the winter unless they have to be."

"I don't plan on staying long." I resisted the urge to peek inside my bag to check on Fernando. How would I explain a frog leaping out? The fewer questions, the better.

"Do you have family here?"

All right. Enough with the third degree from the peanut gallery. I drummed my fingers on the counter. "Just passing through, is all." It came out with more bite than I'd intended. I took a large mouthful of coffee, composing myself. I was overreacting, getting annoyed for no reason. The girl was probably just bored out of her skull, making conversation with the only customer in the place. As a rule, people in this town were chatty and friendly; she likely couldn't help it.

"I'm sorry," I said. "I guess I'm just a little cranky this morning." I lifted my cup and took a sip. "This is my first coffee of the day."

She handed me my sandwich with a smile. "No problem. I understand how that goes."

Did she? At her age, I only understood milk and cookies. "Thanks. I'm just going to run to the restroom, and then I'll be out of your hair."

I went into the bathroom with my coffee and sandwich, which of course didn't look the least bit odd. I had to try feeding Fernando, and I didn't want to go back to Violet's to do it in case I had to swing by the pet store afterward.

Once inside, I made sure the door was locked, then set my cup on the corner table next to the hand lotion and extra roll of toilet paper. I unzipped my purse and was relieved to find my little guy blinking up at me, safe and sound.

I tore off a small piece of ham and waved it by his mouth.

Nothing. Then I placed it on the scarf in front of him, hoping his tongue would dart out and snatch it.

"Come on, Fernando. You have to eat something."

I tried again with a bit of egg and got the same results. My meat-loving fiancé wanted nothing to do with either. Now what? I gave it a few minutes while I looked away in case he suffered from stage fright. Maybe he was embarrassed to eat in front of me in this body.

When I turned back, the grub was still untouched, and now my purse smelled like a fast-food joint. I sighed and tossed the pieces in the trash. Next up on the menu: frog chow.

I polished off the rest of the sandwich and chugged half my coffee before exiting the restroom. If I thought the girl had been giving me questioning looks before… I gave her a little wave as I passed by.

"You ate your breakfast in the bathroom?"

"Um, nope. It's in my purse." I patted it lightly. "Have a great day."

I stepped back out into the blinding sun, made even more so by the reflection off all the snowbanks. I wish I would've remembered to grab that pair of sunglasses off Violet's dresser.

I shielded my eyes and took the few paces over to Murphy's. I used to love this store. It was where I'd picked out my first—and last—fish, thanks to my sister. I hadn't wanted to subject another living thing to her recklessness. And here I thought she'd grown out of that stage. Ha! No, she'd just moved up higher on the food chain.

A bell above the door dinged when I opened it. It was a much more pleasant way of alerting a customer than hurling mugwort in their face. I gave the place a once-over; besides the kitty litter stacked up against a different wall, things were exactly how they'd been thirteen years earlier. That seemed to be the theme here. Was the town stuck in a time warp?

Unlike the coffee house, there were several shoppers inside. I nodded to a couple then made my way to the back. When I passed the terrariums, housing an entire army of tree frogs, the breakfast sandwich churned in my stomach. The thought of Fernando in one of those things made me want to retch. I had to leave the area before I got the insane urge to free them all. Maybe they were also the result of Violet's handiwork. Maybe *all* these animals in here were really humans. *Gah!* I was starting to lose it.

"Can I help you?"

The lady stocking heat lamps appeared to be observing my moral dilemma. Or my psychotic episode. Either way, it wouldn't be long before I was referred to as the out-of-town pariah.

"Yes, you can," I said, going up to her. "Do you carry frog food?"

She just stared at me. Was it that outlandish of a question? Last I checked, we were in a pet store. I cleared my throat, and she snapped out of it.

"I'm sorry, dear. What were you saying now? You'll have to forgive me, but you look awfully familiar."

Hmm, this again. But I did have to admit that she looked familiar as well. Vaguely. Which wasn't unusual, considering she'd probably lived here the entire time I had. I was well aware that I'd probably be running into people who knew me from my past life, but I was hoping to keep the socializing to a minimum. I wasn't here for a reunion.

"I was asking about frog food. Frog pellets or something like that? I didn't see it on the shelf."

"What kind of frog do you have?"

"An enchan—um, I mean an Ecuadorian one." Dang, that'd almost slipped out.

"An Ecuadorian frog?" She scrunched up her face, tapping a

long nail on her chin. "And where exactly did you purchase this particular species? I do hope not off the black market." She frowned at me. "I trust you're aware there's a serious illegal wildlife trade problem? Exotic animals are being sold—"

I held up my hand before she went any further. "It's nothing like that, believe me."

"So then where did you purchase it?"

"Actually, it's a friend's. I'm frog-sitting while they're away."

"And they didn't leave you any food?" She tsked.

I was just digging myself into a deeper hole. "I think he must've eaten it all before I arrived. He's quite the big boy." I chuckled, but she was not amused. "And well, I can't find any more, so if you could just point me toward the frog chow, I can be on my way." *Thanks, Violet. You're turning me into a liar now.* And to top it off, I was probably going to be turned in for frog abuse, along with my imaginary friend. Or worse. I could have my "illegal" animal confiscated. I was beginning to sweat, which probably just made me look guilty. "Um, if you're not sure, I can ask someone else. Not a problem."

"Follow me." She waved me even farther back as my heart pounded harder. Where was she taking me? Was there a special room for suspicious people? I glanced toward the front entrance; I could make a quick getaway if necessary.

"Are you okay, dear? You look a little pale."

I let out a rush of air when she led me to a back register. "I'm fine." Paranoid but fine.

She logged in to the store computer then scrolled her finger over the screen. "Do you by chance have a picture of this frog?" I shook my head. "What color is it?"

"Um, green?"

"You're not sure?"

"Well, funny thing. He's kind of like a chameleon, changing shades to blend in." I imagined he was either bubblegum or hot pink, depending on which scarf he was currently nestled against.

One look at her face and I knew that was absolutely the wrong thing to say. She resembled a Shar-Pei. "That is nothing like we would sell here, and I can assure you we're a reputable dealer. Are you *positive* you're not in possession of an exotic—"

"Well, well, well. Lookie who decided to show her face around here again."

That icy voice made the hairs on the back of my neck stand up straighter than any below-zero day. In fact, it froze my entire body into position. I was in no hurry to turn around and subject my eyes to her ghastly face again.

The saleslady was no longer focused on me but giving a nasty glare to the horridness I knew stood behind me. "Misty! What did I tell you about bringing that snake in here? You scare my customers half to death with that thing."

Snake?

As the woman waggled her finger with a stern expression, her identity shot back to me, her authoritative manner jogging my memory. But even though it was a pleasant memory, that didn't overshadow the vile one behind me. Or should I say, vile person? Misty Evans.

A triangular head poked over my shoulder, and I screamed.

"Misty!" Mrs. Swanson barked again.

I was paralyzed. The snake slithered down my purse strap, and I noticed in absolute horror that I hadn't zipped it up all the way. Holy corolla. Didn't snakes eat…? That jostled me into action. It was as if my feet grew springs, and I vaulted up and away, my heart jackhammering my ribs.

That snake. Her snake. That freaking snake tried to eat my fiancé! I quickly zipped my bag closed and held it tightly against me.

My eyes locked into Misty's beady ones, and I shuddered.

"Sorry, Mrs. Swanson." Misty gave me a 'sorry not sorry' slimy smile that matched her snake's. "He means no harm. I'll make sure to keep him better contained."

Baloney sausage. Misty was such a con artist. Mrs. Swanson crossed her arms. Judging by the look on her face, she didn't believe the little scammer either. It was bad enough the nice woman had to deal with Misty during her school years, but now she had to as an adult too. Major downside to a small town— everyone was close enough to be family, but not every member of your family was a good egg. Or in Misty's case, some were just plain rotten.

"I've had to warn you too many times. Next time, keep it at home."

Misty pointed to the door and said in a sickly sweet tone, "But Mrs. Swanson, your sign says pets are welcome."

"I meant of the well-behaved fur and feather variety."

Misty shrugged, walking away while petting her snake. My heart was still racing.

"Sorry about that." Mrs. Swanson stepped from behind the computer and pulled me into a hug. "Sammara Hain. It's so wonderful to see you again."

I was embarrassed that I hadn't recognized my former beloved elementary teacher. But in my defense, she'd lost about fifty pounds and cut about ten inches off her hair, along with changing it to a more flattering darker tone. She looked amazing.

"Hi, Mrs. Swanson. I didn't recognize you until"—I nodded toward Misty—"you yelled at her." The more things changed, the more they stayed the same.

She laughed. "I couldn't pinpoint who you were at first either. Senior brain and all."

"Nonsense. You're not old. You look fantastic, better than ever."

"How kind of you, dear." She clasped her hands around my arms. "My, my, my, just look how lovely you are. All grown-up. Have you moved back home?"

"Oh no, just paying a visit to my sister."

"That's certainly long overdue."

"Yes, ma'am." It sounded like a scolding to me. She waved her hand with a smile, returning behind the counter. "Speaking of, have you seen Violet recently... like in the past twelve hours?" I nibbled my bottom lip.

She raised an eyebrow. "Lost your sister?"

"Not exactly. I came into town last night, and it seems she's avoiding me."

"Hmm. No, I haven't seen her since I stopped by last week to pick up some thank-you cards." She paused. "But you know, if there's a problem you can come to me. I've always had your back, Samm."

"I know, thank you. Oh, and by the way, I go by Eve now, not Samm."

"Hmm."

I did believe she'd always looked out for me. I trusted her then, and I trusted her now. As much as I could, at least. Like everyone else in the town, she hadn't known the real reason I'd left Bigfoot Bay all those years back. It was a common belief that my parents had separated, and I had gone to live with my dad in Chicago while my mom stayed here with Violet. Then when I was eighteen, my parents reconciled and my dad returned, but I chose to stay in Illinois.

Mrs. Swanson, like all the others, didn't know that I came from a magical family, that my madly-in-love parents had to split up before anyone got hurt. But since she had also doubled as a school recess supervisor, she'd witnessed the daily devious behavior of Misty Evans, usually directed toward me. At least up until the day I left.

Wait a minute. "Mrs. Swanson, what in the world are you doing working here? Shouldn't you be in school?"

She grinned wide. "I don't just work here, dear. I retired from teaching and bought the place from Mr. Murphy. It's my new adventure, and I couldn't be more thrilled."

"Wow, good for you. That's awesome." I flashed back to her always bringing animals into the classroom. One day a bunny, the next a Guinea pig until we seemed to have more class pets than students.

I felt a burning sensation on my back, and I glanced over my shoulder, gripping my purse harder. I couldn't spot Misty anywhere, but I sensed her still lurking about. This was no place for Fernando.

"Pay no mind to that troublemaker. All bark and no bite, she is. She's always around wreaking havoc somewhere."

It wasn't me I was worried about.

"Now, about that frog…"

After ten minutes of respectfully declining her offer to come out and identify the frog and convincing her that my "friend" would never ever obtain a pet illegally, I found myself juggling an assortment of crickets and mealworms. Did I mention they were fresh? *Really* fresh.

"Don't you have something, um, less alive? Or maybe freeze-dried?"

Mrs. Swanson shook her head. "A diet of fresh insects is much healthier. Frogs are carnivores, you know, which means they're also predators."

"Okay," I relented. No biggie, right?

I paid for the bag of froggy delicacies then promised to visit her at least once again before I left. I was eager to get back and get his belly filled. I almost made it out too, until I felt the overwhelming need to take a decontamination shower.

"Leaving so soon? I'm hurt you didn't say goodbye."

Her oily presence coated me like sludge. I turned around. "Yes, Misty, I'm leaving. This isn't a laundromat. People come in, buy something, then leave."

"But we barely had a chance to catch up. What's it been—thirteen years?"

The snake coiled around her hair bun, its creepy slitted pupils leering at me. To say it was unsettling was grossly underplaying it.

I dropped my gaze from the reptile's diabolical eyes to hers. "And I'm sure another thirteen won't kill us." She smirked, and I realized that I felt more comfortable making eye contact with the snake. "Well, I'd like to say it's been nice, but my parents taught me not to lie."

"Oh, I'm sure your parents taught you much more than that."

What did *that* mean? Forget it. I wasn't going to worry about it. I put my hand on the door to push it open, but her giant palm slammed against it.

"Excuse me?"

"We really should get together while you're in town. Me, you, your sister. That is if you can find her."

"Are you implying something or just wasting my time?"

Her grin was so crooked, it bordered on threatening. "You hurt my feelings. I'd expect this behavior out of Violet—she's always picking a fight with me—but you? You're more of a flight kind of girl."

I sighed, her nearness making me gag. Not to mention how nerve-racking it was having the snake within striking distance.

"Then it should come as no surprise I want to leave. Step out of my way."

"Or what?"

"*Or what?* What are we back in grade school?"

"No, if we were, you'd have your sister around to fight your battles."

A shiver crept up my spine when the snake inched a little lower down the side of her head. I took a step back, nearly falling into a stroller.

"Girls," Mrs. Swanson hissed. "You're making a scene." Her hushed voice and clenched jaw were directed toward Misty, even if she was addressing the both of us. "Kindly stop right now."

"Of course, Mrs. Swanson. We were just chatting. I wouldn't dream of causing a disturbance in your store."

"No, you never do."

As the two went back and forth, I noticed we had an audience. A handful of customers had stopped to watch. Great. I didn't understand why Mrs. Swanson even allowed Misty to continue coming into her store. If she owned the place, she had the right to refuse entry.

"Like I was just telling Misty, I really need to be running along." I held up my bugs. "Thanks so much for your time, Mrs. Swanson. It was great seeing you again."

"You too, dear."

This time when I pushed open the door, nothing got in my way. I hightailed it out of there, expecting to be followed and harassed Misty-style, but to my surprise, I made it back to Violet's store without any hassle. On the flip side, walking alone only gave me more opportunity to stew.

By the time I keyed open the door, I was spitting fire. How could I let Misty rattle my chains again after all these years? No doubt she smelled the fear on me, but that was due to her evil companion. I wondered just how tough she'd be without it?

I went in, swatting the herbs aside and cursing my sister. My blood had reached its boiling point. I shouldn't have had to be there dealing with any of this. I was newly engaged and should've been flying high, not encountering past demons.

I raised my fist in the air. "You're screwing up my life, Violet!"

I'd been yelling that so many times I needed to record it and play it on repeat. That way my energy could be conserved for more important things.

Fernando.

I rushed to the bathroom and opened my purse, letting him hop into the bathtub. Just as I pictured, he was shocking pink but quickly dulled to an ivory tone.

"Here you go." I dumped out some of the bugs near his head. *"Bon appetit."*

I sat and watched. He appeared to be snubbing his nose at me if that were possible. *Sorry, Fernando. I didn't mean to upset your delicate sensibilities.*

"Please, just try," I begged. "I know it's not filet mignon, but it's still meat, right? You might like it." I urged him to reach out his tongue and snatch one. I desperately needed him to eat. Doing so would even outweigh the ick factor of kissing him when he was human again. That was what full bottles of mouthwash were for. "Please, Fernando. You *have* to eat."

Or did he? I still wasn't clear on how enchantment affected your metabolism. As if responding to my ponderings, he leaped far away from his meal.

The crickets and worms seemed to be having their own dance party now that they had cause for celebration. I would too if I'd escaped the fate of being someone's breakfast. Any moment now, I expected the music to start. Note to self: Scrub out the tub ASAP.

I lifted Fernando out of the tub and collected all the creepy crawlies back into the bag. I'd return them to the pet store because it was too cold to let them go outside. Just because I was prepared to offer them up as nourishment didn't mean I was cruel.

As I was cleaning up, a memory came pouring back that had nothing to do with bathtubs and everything to do with my annoyance at my sister. "I hope you're enjoying this, Violet," I muttered. "As if it weren't bad enough when you changed my brand-new bike into a stalk of broccoli just because I refused to let you ride it. First of all"—my voice rose higher—"I didn't let you ride it because you had it in your head that you could fly, and I didn't want you riding it off a cliff. And second, I hate broccoli. The very least you could've done was turn it into a hot fudge sundae!"

Argh. I slammed the bleach down and stomped out of the room, making sure to watch the ground beneath me as I worked out my tantrum.

I could not even begin to imagine how the rest of my day would play out.

CHAPTER FOUR

"*S*amm?"

I froze mid-stomp when I caught sight of the strawberry blonde curls, the sylphlike woman standing right inside the doorway. My eyes widened. "Sage?" She looked exactly the same, only now she was more than a decade older. "Sage!" I shrieked, dashing over and wrapping my arms around her.

"Did I interrupt something? You didn't look too happy before you saw me."

"Well, I recently had a run-in with a revolting creature and, oh, a snake too. And I had to scrub—never mind all that." I was speaking as if we'd only been apart for thirteen hours, not years. I pulled back and looked her over. "Wow! You have not changed a bit."

She smiled. "Neither have you." She twirled my hair around her finger, the purple chunk of strands residing underneath the rest of my pale locks. "I'm glad to see you still have this. I always thought it was so beautiful."

I snorted. "As if I could change it. I've never found a dye

that can take to it more than a day or two." I was born with the violet hair streaks, yet *Violet* had hair the color of a blood moon. Go figure. "So apparently, neither of us have changed since eight grade. What do you think that says about us?"

She gave me one of her dazzling smiles, the kind that melted my heart and made me realize how much I'd missed her. "It means we'll stay young forever."

I couldn't believe she was right here in front of me. The closest friend I'd ever had. "Oh, Sage. I've missed you so much."

"Hmm. I wouldn't have guessed that." She picked at her nails. "Since I never heard from you again."

I suddenly felt as small as Fernando. *Fernando*. Shoot! Where was he? "I know. I'm a horrible friend and I don't expect you to forgive me. It might be hard to understand, but I just wanted to start over and forget my old life."

Sage gave me a playful shove. "Yet somehow I survived."

"But I never forgot you. I swear I didn't."

"I know. I'm just messing with you. Kind of."

Sage was the only soul who knew about my family—to an extent. She was there with me that day on school grounds and witnessed everything that went down with Misty. She knew my family was "eccentric" and why I left town, and that it had nothing to do with my parents' so-called separation. But what she didn't know was that we were witches. How would you drop something like that on your best friend without expecting her to run away screaming?

I tugged her over to the couch, unsure if her inability to hold a grudge appeased my guilt or worsened it. "So, what are you doing here?" I asked. "I only arrived late last night."

Her lips curved up, her enormous emerald eyes sparkling. "And already you're causing a stir."

"What?"

She pulled a paper bag out of her purse. "I was coming to

drop these off for Violet, hoping to exchange them for some chamomile tea. But on the way over, I heard from Susan who heard from Callie that you were back in town."

I rolled my eyes. Gotta love Bigfoot Bay. I took the bag and opened it. "What's in here?"

"Fresh blueberries, just picked this morning."

Her purse was still open, and I spotted her phone. It was the same as mine. "You wouldn't happen to also have a charger in there, would you? My phone is dead and I forgot to bring mine."

"Nope, sorry."

"No problem." I got up and set the bag behind the counter. "I'll get your tea. Violet won't mind."

Since Sage was female and the sweetest thing on the planet, Violet didn't hold it against her that she was human. In fact, they've always been friendly with each other. I never had to worry about Sage's safety around my sister.

I scanned the jars of leaves on the shelves. If chamomile wasn't out here, I could always check the supply closet. Fortunately, the lids were clearly labeled since I wouldn't know wintergreen from wolfsbane.

Ah, here it is. I plunked the jar off the top shelf and shook some into a tin. "Is that enough?" I asked.

"Plenty. I've been swamped lately and it's affecting my sleep. This is the only thing that works for me. I swear it's sleeping dust."

It probably was.

"Will Violet be back soon?"

"I'm not sure…" I put the jar back in its rightful place. "But I'll make sure to give her the—wait a minute. It's March. How did you pick the blueberries this morning?"

"I grow them in my greenhouse all year round. Easy peasy."

"Easy for you, maybe. You're the Plant Whisperer."

I'd always joked that she liked plants better than people., and they obviously returned her affection since they perked up in her presence. To the point that it was freaky. I recalled second period English and the sad bouquet of flowers that sat on Mrs. Wilson's desk, but whenever Sage entered the classroom, they looked less droopy. Happy even, if flowers could look happy. The first time it happened, I thought I was hallucinating from skipping lunch that day, but after a dozen more times, I just chalked it up to a knack of hers.

I handed Sage her chamomile. "Bring me up to date. Tell me everything. What's been going on that you're so busy?"

"Studying. Lots and lots of studying. I've been finishing up my coursework in the botany and herbology program, and between that and keeping up with the greenhouse, it's been nonstop. Oh, and the winter farmers' market every week... can't forget about that. But I wouldn't slow down for anything. I love it all."

"That's so great, Sage." I was truly happy for her, even if she made me feel like a slacker without meaning to. I still hadn't decided what I wanted to be when I grew up. "But it sounds like all work and no play. What about your love life? Seeing anyone?"

She waved her hand. "No time for that. Plants are more interesting anyway. Hey, you should come to my booth at the market next week! It's every Thursday morning by the marina." She narrowed her eyes. "You *will* still be here, right?"

"Um..." That was six days from now. I sure hoped not.

"Samm! How can you even think of leaving again so soon? This town is happy you're back. Can't you feel it? You're meant to be here. And besides, I think you owe me lots of catching up."

"Actually, I go by Eve now."

"Pfft. Not as far as I'm concerned." She stared me down. "And stop evading."

"I'm not evading anything. It's just that I don't know yet how long I'll be here. Honest. See, I have a fiancé now and—"

She grabbed my shoulders. "What? A fiancé?" I nodded. "And you're just telling me this now?"

"Well, yeah. It's pretty quick, considering we only reunited twenty min—"

"Who is it?" she demanded.

"No one you—"

"Did you set a date yet?" I opened my mouth. "How long have you been together?" I closed my mouth. No use getting a word in until she finished. "Is that why you came back? Come on, tell me *everything*."

Her enthusiasm made me smile. "I would, but that's kinda hard to do when you're not letting me talk." She humphed, crossing her arms, then gestured for me to continue. "His name is Fernando. We met at a Chicago food fair. Been together six months. No date yet but soon. Really soon. It was so spur-of-the-moment, I'm still picking out the ring."

"Ooh… Fernando. Sounds exotic."

She didn't know the half of it. I scoured the room. Where was he anyway? I'd gotten so preoccupied with Sage I'd never made sure he was okay.

"I hope it's not inappropriate to say, in light of your recent engagement," Sage continued, "and I know it might sound silly because you were just kids, but I always thought you'd end up with… Are you looking for something?"

I jerked my head up. "Give me just a minute, okay? I really have to go to the bathroom."

I darted into the bedroom and checked around. Nothing. Then the bathroom. No sign there either. If I wasn't willing to stick him in one of those glass cages—and I wasn't—then I had to make sure I got the place frog-proofed.

Upon leaving the room, I noticed the blueberry bag rustling behind the counter.

"I thought you had to use the bathroom?" Oh shoot, I forgot to flush the toilet.

"False alarm." Technically, I hadn't lied. I said I had to go to the bathroom, and I did go in there.

I casually sidled over, aware of Sage's eyes on me, and peeked in the paper bag. Fernando had burrowed inside and was perched atop the berries, shaded a matching deep purple. I crumbled it closed then backed up enough to bend down and slip it into the closet.

"You okay?"

"Yeah, why do you ask?"

"For starters, you're acting cra—" My cell rang and I jumped. "Didn't you say your phone was dead?"

I had a bout of nervous laughter. "It's been acting up lately." I gaped at it like it was going to sprout horns. I wouldn't have been surprised if it had.

"Aren't you going to answer it?"

I checked the screen—another unknown number. Sure, what the heck. "Hello?"

"Grandma?"

I pulled the phone from my ear and scrunched up my face. Then I yelled, "Do I sound like a grandma to you?" The call dropped then the battery lost its life. I rolled my eyes and slammed it down.

"Wow, that was harsh. You probably just traumatized some sweet little kid."

I glanced up and sighed. I'd never be able to convince her that it was more likely a spooky ghost boy. "Yeah, I guess I've been a bit out of sorts lately."

"Pre-wedding jitters. I get it. You probably have tons to do." Her expression told me she wanted to believe that was the cause, but she wasn't fully convinced. "There's not anything you're not telling me, is there?"

I put my hand over my heart. "I'm overwhelmed, that's it. Heart promise." It may have been a generic answer, but it wasn't a dishonest one.

"Hmm. Okay. Busy or not, I'll still help out when I can. You know, to make things a little less stressed for you."

"Nah, I'd rather you focus on school, but I appreciate the offer." She frowned, and I hoped she hadn't thought I was brushing her off. "But I'll let you know for sure," I added. "Fernando and I are keeping things really low-key anyway."

"When are you and Violet going shopping?"

"Shopping?"

"Yes, silly. Dress shopping and all that wedding-ish stuff. Isn't that why you're here, to go over the plans with your maid of honor?"

"Violet's not my maid of honor."

"But she's your sister!"

"We're not exactly close, as you know…" Of course! It was so clear to me now. I'd made some new friends over the years, but no one compared to Sage. "You're the only one I want standing next to me at the altar. Well, besides Fernando." I smiled. "But only if you're okay with coming to Chicago and—"

"Eek! Yes, I'll be your maid of honor!" She wrapped me in a full body chokehold. "What can I do?"

"Remember, I'll let you know. We haven't set a date yet."

"But you said it'd be soon."

"No, I said we'd set a date soon, not that the wedding would be soon."

She bounced around the shop. "There's so much to get

done. We should at least go dress shopping." This was quickly spiraling out of control. How could I think about dresses when my fiancé was too small to wear a tux? "The look on your face... As your maid of honor, I gotta ask—are you sure Fernando is the right guy?"

My jaw dropped. "Of course, he is."

"I'm sorry. I didn't mean to upset you."

"It's fine. You didn't."

She eyed me over then grabbed a pen and a piece of sample stationery off the counter and scribbled down a number. "Call me. Tomorrow. I have to get back to the books."

"Okay."

"Promise you'll call."

"I promise."

She was giving me another crushing hug when we were hit with a blast of cold air.

"Knock knock."

I felt Sage tense. We both swiveled toward the front door where a woman was poking her head into the shop. *Dang it.* I'd forgotten to lock up after Sage arrived. I was not equipped to deal with Violet's customers. I couldn't talk soap or tea or fancy paper.

"Sage. How lovely to see you again."

"Clarisse," she replied through clenched teeth. I scrunched up my face, confused as all get out over her reaction.

The mystery lady came inside and closed the door, sidestepping the herbs hanging down. Ha. Some security system.

"Can I help you?" I asked.

The thirtysomething woman appeared to be casing the place. Very attractive with perfectly styled platinum hair and skyscraper heels, she stuck out like a werewolf at a bald men's convention. Who dressed to the nines on a weekday morning in Bigfoot Bay?

"Yes, Clarisse. Do you need something?" Sage stood with her arms crossed, tapping her foot. "I'm sure there are closer places to buy your bath bubbles."

Clarisse ignored her, turning her focus on me. I felt a chill which made me question if the door had opened again. I instantly disliked her without a rational reason.

She smiled, revealing painted white teeth that were as phony as her fake warmth. "And you are?"

"Eve."

"This is Violet's sister." Sage smirked. "Otherwise known as Samm."

I swore the woman's smile grew so high it extended to her forehead. She couldn't hide her uncrinkled eyes, though. Judging by the shards shooting from them, I was pretty sure she didn't like me either, and it was all based on learning my identity.

What the heck was going on?

"Samm. I've heard *so* much about you. How nice to finally put a face to the name."

"Same face, different name. I go by Eve now. And I'm sorry, but I don't know a thing about you." I glanced at Sage. "What am I missing here?"

Clarisse waved her red dragon-lady nails around and laughed. Good grief, she had a handful of mini-weapons at her disposal. "I'm sure you'll hear all about me soon enough." She laughed harder, turning on the charm. "And don't believe a word of it."

"Okay," I said. My eyes darted back and forth between them. I wasn't a fan of being kept in the dark.

"Is Violet here? I dropped by to pick up an order."

"Oh, would you look at the time. I'd better vamoose," Sage

said, then whispered in my ear, "Remember sweet old Mr. Jones?" I nodded. He'd lived in the monstrous lakefront mansion on the outskirts of town and had more money than all the residents put together, including the millionaires. "Well, that's his not-so-sweet, not-so-old surviving widow. Enough said." Sage blew me a kiss then flurried out the door as if the wind carried her.

Mr. Jones's recent passing had made the news, and so had the fact that he'd remarried a couple of years prior to someone young enough to be his daughter. A woman who now had complete control of his entire estate. Wow.

"So, Clarisse… what's this about an order?"

"Yes, a special tea." I didn't like the way she held the store under scrutiny, like she was planning on coming back later to rob it. *Yeah, okay, Eve.* Like she was going to clear out all the soap bars and teacups. *Stop being so paranoid.* But then again… Sage had a problem with her so that had to mean something.

"You know, Violet's not here at the moment. Maybe you could come back?"

"No, that wouldn't be convenient. I'm sure it's here somewhere. I'll just poke around a bit."

"I don't think that's a good—"

Another cold blast through the front door. Had Sage returned? No, it was someone just as willowy but much shorter. Her apple-cheeked face looked very…

"Amy?"

She returned my stare for a few beats before her eyes also widened in recognition.

"Samm? Is that you?"

"It's Eve now, but yep, it's me." She rushed over and gave me a squeeze. "What are you doing back?"

"Visiting my sister."

Amy was a few years younger than me, the same age as

Violet, and she was sweeter than a bowl of sherbet punch. Which made it all the crazier to know that she shared the same blood as Misty. Yep, they were sisters and couldn't have been more different than sunshine and darkness.

"How've you been? Violet talks about you all the time."

"Then I apologize for the bad language."

She laughed, flicking her wrist. "Oh, you. Such a kidder. You know, it wasn't too long ago when we sat right there, sharing a cup of tea." Amy pointed to the corner table. "She told me how much she misses you."

More like missed blowing up my stuff. But leave it to Amy to put a positive spin on it. She spread cheerfulness wherever she went, unlike her sibling who spread pestilence.

"Ready to move home?" Amy asked. "You have to be tired of the big city by now."

"Nope. I love Chicago. So, what about you? What have you been up to?"

"Oh, same old, same old. Not quite as adventurous as you, still living in the same house I was born and raised. Hey, are you going to the festival tonight?" *Festival... festival...* The barista had also asked me that. "Remember? The ice festival?"

Oh right! An image instantly popped into my mind, showing huge ice sculptures, tunnels, slides. It was an extremely popular winter attraction, and people came from all around to see it. Depending on the weather, it was open for a good solid month or so. During that time, the entire lakefront was mobbed, almost as if it were tourist season, and when it was over, the town reverted back to the locals until late spring.

It was one of my favorites growing up. I had never missed it when I lived here.

"That's tonight? I thought it would've been over by now."

"Yep, tonight. It's the grand reopening. They had to shut it down for a while due to the unseasonably warm weather, but now it's back. Probably not for long, though. I have to make sure I go early and get some of Violet's cinnamon hot chocolate before it's gone."

"Hot chocolate?"

Amy nodded, rubbing her stomach. "She has a stand there, and I swear, I wait all year for it. You should convince her to start offering it at her shop. I haven't been able to. She says people will want it more when they can only get it once a year. Do you know when she's planning to arrive?"

"No, I—"

The screech reminded me that we weren't the only two in the place. How had I forgotten about Clarisse?

"What in the devil is that?!"

I whipped my head around to see Clarisse hopping back and forth like she was dodging a mouse. The storage closet door was also cracked open.

Son of a gargoyle. I hurried over and peered inside. If that woman had spiked him with one of her stilettos... I couldn't even finish the thought. I scanned the floor and didn't see him, which I took as a good sign. He was probably hiding somewhere. Unless he was hiding and wounded. Ugh. Visiting hours were now over. I liked Amy just as much as I distrusted Clarisse, but it was time for both of them to go.

Wait a flippin' minute. "What were you doing back here?"

Clarisse smoothed down her pencil skirt. "You need to tell Violet to call in an exterminator. I just saw a giant roach."

I rolled my eyes. "There're no roaches in here. Now, what were you doing in there?"

"Why, looking for my order, of course."

I shut the door. "This room is for employees only." I ran my hand over the Employees Only sign in case it wasn't clear enough for her.

"That may pertain to some customers, but I've been allowed in there before. Nothing to get in a tizzy about."

I kept my mouth shut because how was I to know whether or not that was true? Just because my gut was telling me she was a blatant liar didn't mean she was. But on the other hand, just because she could buy a small country, didn't mean that entitled her to free rein wherever she went.

"I'll let Violet know you stopped by, and you'll get your order as soon as possible. That's the best I can do. Now, if you'll kindly leave, I have things to take care of."

I was past the point of caring if I offended her. Especially when she gave me that cunning little smile. *Wow, you've really taken a shine to her, Eve.*

"Fair enough. I'm sure I'll see you around... Eve."

That jolted me. Clarisse was the only one in town so far who'd called me Eve upon my request, and that disturbed me on a level I didn't understand. But then everything about her had that yuck factor. I was relieved to see her leave.

As soon as Ms. I'll See My Way Out left the shop, I turned to Amy. "What is up with that woman? I don't like her nosing around like that."

Amy shrugged. "Who knows? I should get going too, though. How long will you be in town?"

"I'm not sure."

"Just don't leave without saying goodbye."

"I won't." She gave me a quick hug and was almost out the door when I stopped her. "Wait! Why'd you stop by?"

Amy slapped her forehead. "Silly me." She opened her purse and pulled out a wrapped-up loaf of bread. "I came to drop off some of my chocolate chip banana bread. Violet loves it."

"How sweet of you." I bit my cheeks, questioning the validity of that statement. But hey, for all I knew, Violet had already chowed through a dozen. "I'll make sure she gets it." I made a note to add it to the other three in the fridge.

When Amy was gone, I locked the door, triple-checked it, then turned the sign to CLOSED.

I immediately went to the closet, tossing the loaf on the table along the way. "Fernando?"

I opened the door, spotting him clear as day on the floor, munching on blueberries. He appeared unharmed, no heel marks on his back. I turned the paper bag upside down and only a few berries tumbled out.

My mouth dropped as I watched him scarf up the remaining ones, his eyes closing with each swallow. If I hadn't seen it for myself, I wouldn't have believed it.

My uber-alpha, carnivore fiancé who practically devoured his steaks raw was sating his appetite on fruit.

Seriously?

After the initial shock, I squealed. Who cared what he ate? The point was, he ate!

I scooped him up and did a happy dance. It was one less thing to worry about. As long as I had blueberries, he wouldn't starve.

My slick moves must've impressed him because I swore he smiled. Or maybe he was laughing at me because a noise bubbled out. Or he was giddy over a full belly. How would I know? I wasn't fluent in Frog Speak.

"Get used to dancing, big guy, because soon we'll be doing it at our wedding."

The thought both encouraged and disheartened me. It'd been barely half a day since the nightmare began, but it felt like a year. I was completely at the mercy of my lunatic sister. There was only one thing I could control right now, and I was going to take full advantage of it.

"Let's get you some more blueberries. What do you say?"

I took his croak as a yes, so I snuggled him back into my purse. It was a short walk to the market, and I was going to make sure we always had a steady supply of berries on hand.

I zipped up my coat, and with him securely tucked against my side, I slipped out the door. It only took two steps before I'd almost collided with the most handsome face I'd ever seen. *Sorry, Fernando.* I patted my bag gently. Second most handsome, I meant to say.

Wait a minute. I knew that face. Amber eyes gazed back at me, and my pulse skyrocketed.

"Wow, Sammi. It really is you."

How many more surprises could my heart possibly take?

CHAPTER FIVE

"Um." I swallowed hard. "It's Eve now."

Really? After all this time, the first thing I did was correct him?

He smiled, reminding me how much I loved his pointed eye teeth. It was a strange fixation, but I melted whenever I saw them. *Used to melt.*

While I was caught off guard, he swooped in and embraced me. "I just can't believe it's you. You're really home. It's been so long."

That snapped me out of it enough to push back gently, placing a respectable distance between us. I hoped that Fernando remained clueless and couldn't sense my reaction to another man. But it wasn't just any man... And he hadn't even been one when I'd left, but he was all man now. No boy lingered in him. And like everyone else in this town, he looked better. Much better. *Stop it, Eve.*

"Griffin."

My skin tingled, and I took another step back. *Think of the frog, think of the frog I mean, fiancé, darn it!*

Once there was enough space and cool air circulating freely between us, it was like a fresh slap in the face. Exactly what I needed. Yeah, I just needed to regain my senses. Griffin was a slice of my past, we shared a history, and that was all. He was a certain comfort that could only be found in a childhood crush, and I got tangled up in the familiarity.

"You look incredible," he said. "I used to think you were the most beautiful thing in the world, but I obviously hadn't met your future self yet."

My cheeks felt like hot plums. I could've easily expressed the same sentiment to him if it would've been appropriate to do so.

"Well, it's been nice seeing you again." I sucked in a deep breath, relishing the iciness as it entered my lungs. I gave him a little wave and turned to leave.

He caught my arm. "Wait! You're leaving already?"

I paused, biting down on my lower lip. What was I so afraid of? If I was secure in my current relationship, I should've been able to have a conversation with my ex-boyfriend without any problem.

"Since we already said hi, I just thought…" Thought what exactly? I wouldn't have acted this way with anyone else. Why should he be any different?

"It's been thirteen years and you're walking away without so much as a 'how've you been?'"

"You're right." I faced him with a smile. "So, how've you been?"

"Have dinner with me tonight and find out."

I suddenly felt as if I were plunged into a furnace. "Oh no. I can't do that."

"Why not?"

I made figure eights in the snow with my boot, feeling thirteen all over again. That high you get when your biggest crush asks you to prom? Yeah, I was experiencing some of that right now. Except if I were a teenager, I would've been hugging myself and twirling around like my world had never seen a sunnier day. But we were adults now with responsibilities and commitments.

Out of the corner of my eye, I saw an elderly couple nearby, sitting on a street bench with their Bigfoot Café paper cups cradled in gloved hands, staring straight at us. I imagined them whispering to each other, judging me for getting all flustered by the attractive man in front of me when I already had a perfectly wonderful fiancé hopping around in my purse.

Stupid imagination.

I set aside his dinner question and asked, "Were you coming into the shop to see Violet just now? Because she's not here."

My stomach did a backflip. I didn't peg him for a tea drinker or a frilly stationery writer or a perfumed bath soap kind of guy, so if he was coming to see Violet, did that mean he wanted to *see* her?

Holy crikey. Could they be involved with each other? No. She would've told me. Possibly. It wasn't like my sister and I were best buds here. If they were dating or something... My stomach stepped up the acrobatics, performing a triple aerial and landing in a split.

Okay, I was officially a nutcase. I'd gone from worrying about him asking me out to worrying about him seeing my sister in ten seconds flat.

"Yes, I was coming to Violet's shop." None of it was my business. And since I was engaged, it *really* wasn't my business. "To see you."

I looked up from the elaborate design I'd created on the sidewalk. "To see me? How'd you know..." I chuckled and some of the tension drained away. "Let me guess—my altercation with Misty at the pet store?"

"No, Sage told me you were home when I passed her on the

street a bit ago." My lips flattened. Now, what had made her go and do something like that? "But yeah, I also heard about you and Misty."

"Of course." He laughed, and I averted my eyes from his teeth.

"If you don't want to do dinner, how about coming with me to the ice festival tonight."

"I don't think that'd be a good idea."

"Come on, it'll be fun. I remember how much you loved it, and besides, it'll give us a chance to catch up."

"Griffin, I'm… with someone, and it's serious."

There I'd done it. My conscience was clear. I could've said I was engaged, but I didn't want him thinking I was using that as an excuse due to my lack of a ring.

"I'm not asking you out on a date, Sammi."

"It's Eve. And you're not?"

"No, I'm not." He grabbed hold of my arms. "Look. I'd only like to spend some time with you to see what you've been up to. That's all. No ulterior motive here. I get that we were just kids when you left, but I consider you one of my closest friends."

One of his closest friends that just up and left without even saying goodbye. That couldn't have felt too good. Looking back, it was a crummy thing to do. He excluded this little fact from our conversation, but he didn't have to mention it in words. I could read it on his face.

Great. Now, I felt lower than the lake algae.

"You can even bend my ear all night about this guy you're serious with. If fact, I'll insist upon it. How else am I going to make sure he's good enough for you?"

I sighed, catching a snowflake on the tip of my nose. It was starting to flurry again. It'd be a beautiful night for the festival. "How about I let you know? I'm back in town to spend time with my sister so I'll have to see what's going on with her first."

His lips curved up. "I can live with that."

Yeah, but could Fernando?

After picking up several containers of blueberries and another coffee, I was back in the shop with the front door locked. No more surprises. I was putting my foot down. It wasn't even noon, and I was all tapped out.

"Still hungry?" I let Fernando out of my purse and placed a small berry in front of him, but he ignored it. It looked anemic compared to Sage's, but a blueberry was a blueberry, right?

I dumped out several more, but he just sailed over to a purple blob in the corner. On closer inspection, I noticed it was a lone blueberry from Sage's stash that must've rolled free from the rest. He gobbled it right up.

I rolled my eyes. "Sorry if the store-bought berries aren't up to your high standards." When had my fiancé become such a fruit connoisseur?

Just for the heck of it, I popped one into my mouth. Blech. It tasted like cardboard, probably plucked thousands of miles away while still green, never having a chance to ripen properly. Geez. Now, *I* sounded like a snob.

"All right, Fernando. I'll give you a pass on this one."

My screeching phone had us both leaping to the ceiling. Or maybe he would've done that anyway. He was a frog for flippin' sake. It's what they did.

I dropped my head in my hands. For as long as I lived, I would never get over this. Even when he was human again, would I still look at him and see bulging eyes and springy legs? The continued ringing snapped me somewhat out of my little funk and I focused on annoyance instead. I glowered at my cell like it was the enemy.

Oops, wrong foe.

It wasn't my cursed phone, after all. It was Violet's landline. I begrudgingly dragged myself over and said, "Violet's Soap & Tea Emporium," just in case it was an actual customer.

"Eve, is that you?"

"Mrs. Geller?" My neighbor in Chicago. I was about to ask what in the world she was doing calling Violet's store when I remembered that I'd given her the number. A rancid taste filled my mouth wondering if my apartment had been broken into. "Everything okay?"

"Oh, it's fine. Well, except for the swelling in my ankles. That's been giving me some problems."

"Is that why you called, Mrs. Geller?"

She chuckled. "And I'm considered a senior? You're a young chickadee, and your memory is worse than mine."

I took a deep breath. "So, you are calling about your ankles, then?"

"Follow along with me, Eve," she said slowly. "You asked me to keep an eye on your place, to let you know if anything new happens. Remember that?"

"Of course." I tugged at my hair. "But you said everything's fine."

"It is. Except for my ankles."

Argh. I loved the woman, but a little more time talking to her and I'd wind up bald.

"I'm sorry to hear about your ankles. Are you soaking them in Epsom salt? That seemed to help before."

"I'm doing that as we speak. You're so sweet to be concerned, but I'll be right as rain in no time." *Deep breath. Deep breath.* "But why in Sam Hill are you discussing my ankles when I'm trying to tell you about Fernando's brother?"

"What about his brother?"

"That's what I've been trying to tell you. You really should pay better attention."

My skin was going to rub off my face, but at least it'd match the bald patches on my scalp. "Of course. How silly of me. Please continue."

"He knocked on your door, oh, about fifteen minutes ago."

"How did you know it was his brother?"

"Well, I certainly wasn't going to let some strange man knock on your door without finding out who it was. I went out to see what all the commotion was about."

"You should be more careful, Mrs. Geller."

"Pfft. I can take care of myself. I'm tougher than I look." I smiled. She was right about that. "He told me his name's Sal. A dead ringer for your beau, which kept my suspicion antenna in check. Said he needed to speak with Fernando and assumed he was at your place."

"And you told him...?" I briefly recalled Fernando mentioning a brother, but I'd never met him. In fact, I'd never met any of his family. Just a side effect of a fast-moving relationship, but one I'd remedy as soon as everything was back on track.

"What do you think I told him? I said he wasn't here, and I would know because I know everything that happens on this floor."

"And then what happened?"

"Then he stormed off. I watched through my window as he raced away in Fernando's car."

"What? No, it couldn't have been Fernando's car. That's..." *Not possible because Violet already took off in it.*

She snorted. "You think I don't know that man's car? It's here practically every night."

"Sal could have the same car."

"With the same mean-looking bull bumper sticker?"

"Yes, it's the basketball team. For Chicago. That's not

exactly uncommon around there."

"With the same red Italian horn hanging from the mirror?" Well, they were family… "And the same star-shaped chip on the bottom right of the windshield?"

How in the world…? Oh yeah, she loved her binoculars. I pressed my forehead against the wall to keep it from swimming away with this new information. The possibility of it still being Sal's car had dwindled down to single digits. But it was even more boggling to consider how Fernando's car could be back in Chicago this morning in Sal's possession when it was in Bigfoot Bay only seventeen hours ago in Violet's.

"Can you do me a huge favor?" I asked. "If Sal turns up again, can you give him this same number and tell him to call me? It's really important I speak to him."

"Is there any funny business going on that I should know about? Because I'm not getting involved in—"

"No, Mrs. Geller." At least not in the way she was thinking. "It's nothing like that. Can you please just do this for me? Also, let me know if anything else happens."

After convincing her I wasn't involved in anything shady, she promised to help. I thanked her, hung up the receiver, and rested my hands on the glass counter, attempting to piece everything together. The chocolate chip banana loaf sidetracked me; it had little footprints running up and down its length.

"Fernando!" I tossed the loaf in the trash. "You can't just hop on anything you want."

I found him sitting atop the visitor guest book, blending in with the creamy white pages. I shook my head. How was I supposed to figure this mess out and keep track of him?

All right, back to business. What *did* I have so far? Fernando drove to Violet's shop for reasons unknown, they argued, and then she turned him into Mr. Short, Green, and Bewitched. *Sometimes* green. Right now he resembled a white chocolate frog.

Moving on… After Violet spelled him, she took off in his car and what… drove to Chicago? Is that where she was hiding out right now? And how did Sal end up with the car?

Gah! My brain was going to explode. I had to suck it up and call Sage. I needed help, and she was the only one who could possibly give it. The only problem was, I couldn't tell her everything. She'd never signed up to have a witch for a best friend.

Oh, and there was the little matter of her blabbing to Griffin that I was home. Not that he wouldn't have heard it from the rest of the town anyway, but Sage needn't have told him. She knew I was engaged.

I was dialing her number when I glanced over at Fernando. He was watching me.

"Yello."

"Hey, Sage. It's Eve."

"I know your voice, Samm. What's up?"

She was worse than my mom. "I didn't mention this before because I didn't want to make a big deal about it, but when was the last time you saw Violet?"

"A few days ago. Why, what's wrong?"

"I just really need to see her, and the longer it gets, the more impatient *I* get. I can't hang out here for too long and I really, really need to see her," I repeated. Fernando began leaping around the room, changing from teal to orange to brown depending on what he landed on. It was oddly mesmerizing.

"Samm?"

"What?"

"I was talking to you. Where'd you go?"

I peeled my eyes away. *Stay focused, Eve.* "Just tired, I guess. Or maybe I respond better to Eve."

She huffed into the line. "Whatever. But about Violet… She

71

must've told you something. Didn't you talk to her before you came here?"

"Yes, but when I got here she was gone."

"Now, you're scaring me."

That wasn't my intent. "I'm sure it's nothing bad. Actually, I'm positive it's not." I wrapped the cord around my hand. Who still used corded phones? But it did give me something to do while I considered how much I could divulge and still sound normal. "The truth is, we got into a big fight last night."

"About what?"

"She doesn't approve of Fernando. She asked me to drive out, probably to try and change my mind, but when I did, she wasn't here. She, uh, did some things to him that were pretty cruel, and I think she took off right afterward so she wouldn't have to own up to it. She knew how furious I'd be."

"What'd she do?"

"You know how she can be when she acts without thinking. Now, multiply that by a gazillion. The point is I need to find her so I can make things right with Fernando again."

"Hmm. Are you sure Violet doesn't have a good reason for feeling the way she does about him?"

"Sage! Whose side are you on?"

"Both of yours, because I don't know who this guy is."

"You were excited for me when I first told you."

"Yeah, but then... I don't know. I got a weird vibe from you when you were talking about him."

"That's because I'm stressed to the gills right now!"

"Okay, okay. Settle down." I sat on the floor, cross-legged, and tapped my fingers on my knee. Fernando was off hiding somewhere. "Tell me what I can do."

"You know her better than me at this point. If she were going to lie low for a while, where would she do it?"

"She loves her shop. That's where she'd be."

"I thought you were supposed to be helping me?"

"I'm trying, but what kind of question is that?"

"What if she had a car? Is there any place she ever talked about going? Maybe Milwaukee or Chicago?"

"The only thing Violet likes less than the city is driving in one."

"Just because she doesn't like to do it, doesn't mean she wouldn't. She'll do whatever it takes to avoid me."

"Overreacting much?"

No! I wanted to scream. Nothing about the situation involved me overreacting. If anything, I was making a molehill out of a mountain.

"What about a friend's house? Could she have slept there last night?" I asked calmly.

"Like a slumber party? She's not twelve." Sage giggled, sounding like *she* was twelve. "But, hmm… I do suppose it's a little strange that she never slept in her own bed. You know, maybe she booked a room at the hotel until things with you two settled down. Yeah, I bet that's it. They probably even gave her a free room since they sponsor the ice festival." Her voice perked up. "She'll be back before you know it, especially with the festival tonight. She'd never miss that. Not when people line up to buy her famous hot chocolate."

"Speaking of the ice festival, why'd you tell Griffin I was back?"

"How does that remind you of Griffin? And why are you whispering?"

"He asked me to go there with him."

"That's great! Then you'll also see Violet and everything will get resolved."

"No, it's not great."

"Seriously, Samm. Why are you whispering?"

I didn't know where Fernando was, and I didn't know how

much English he comprehended. He had enough complications to deal with at the moment, and overhearing me talk about my ex-crush shouldn't be one of them, but I also didn't feel right about hiding things from him. I was so torn.

"Never mind," I finally said.

"You're acting bizarre. See what happens when you stay away too long?"

"Or maybe it's because I came back." I noticed the supply closet door cracked open. Hadn't I shut it earlier? "I just want to see Violet, that's all. Then everything will be back to normal again."

"So, then go to the festival with Griffin and that'll happen. He misses you, we all do. Does having a fiancé suddenly mean you can't associate with anyone in your past anymore?"

"You know there's more to it than that. You yourself said you thought Griffin and I would end up together."

"And obviously that didn't happen because you're engaged to someone else. What's the big deal? Go and have some fun. What are you afraid of—rekindling the spark? Are you planning on kissing him afterward?"

"No!" Geez. If Fernando were next to me, I'd be covering his ear holes right now. "I already told Griff I'm in a serious relationship."

"Do you want my opinion? If you were secure in said relationship, you wouldn't even be worrying about this at all."

Was that true? It felt like she'd slipped into my head and was throwing my own thoughts and concerns back at me.

"I guess, but—" A loud crash from the closet had me jumping up.

"What was that?"

"I'm not sure, but I gotta go."

I hung up and bolted to the room. A jar lay broken on the ground in a few large shards. There was a space missing on the top shelf where it must've fallen from. Fernando was sitting nearby, appearing no worse for the wear.

I picked up the pieces. "Did you do this?" Luckily, the jar was empty so there wasn't much of a mess to clean up. The lid stated it was feverfew, which meant nothing to me.

I shooed him out with a slight smile. I couldn't allow him to run wild and go on a destruction spree, but I couldn't deny him a little excitement either. I imagined his current life was pretty dang boring. Hmm. Perhaps, I should reconsider and let him go on a free-for-all inside her shop.

It would serve her right.

I SPENT the next couple hours mulling everything over, and in the end, I called Griffin. I accepted his offer to accompany him to the festival. I'd decided I needed all the allies I could get, especially ones who had an in with local law enforcement. The longer Violet was MIA, the more I'd be in need of reinforcements.

But my fingers were crossed that she would be there, standing behind her booth, even if I wasn't holding my breath.

While I was lying there, staring at the ceiling and contemplating, I came up with the most plausible explanation I could. Violet had to have stolen his car, and Mrs. Geller had to have been mistaken that morning. It was Sal's car she saw, not Fernando's. They were brothers; it only made sense that they would take an interest in similar things. And the chip... well, all it took was a drive behind a dump truck carrying rocks, and a ding in the windshield could happen to anyone.

The most difficult decision of all was figuring out what to do with Fernando. As I spread out on the bed with him snoozing on my stomach, I debated bringing him along. I did not want to leave him alone, but I also couldn't subject him to the cold for long periods. Short stints on a sunny day wrapped up in a scarf was one thing, dark snowy nights quite another when you were cold-blooded.

Or, maybe... I shook my head, lifting him off of me so I could start getting ready. I refused to go down another rabbit hole by questioning if his enchantment somehow enabled him to keep the warm blood of a mammal. It wasn't my spell; I had no way to know exactly what I was dealing with, so why drive myself bonkers with all the what-ifs?

Fernando would be fine for a few hours holed up in Violet's bedroom. I did a thorough check to ensure there was nothing that'd harm him, confirming the bathroom door was tightly shut. I bunched up the blankets to create a cozy den on top of the bed and gave him a fresh bowl of water, even though he had yet to take any interest in it.

"There you are." I placed him in the middle of the blankets. "All good to go."

The knock sounded at six o'clock sharp. Right on time. I brought my fingers to my lips then placed them on top of his head. I headed for the door but not before glancing back. Big mistake. "Please, don't look at me like that. I'm doing this to help you. Help us. My cowardly sister can't hide away forever, and I'm going to find her and make her fix this. I promise."

He blinked twice then pivoted, obviously preferring the wall to me. I almost canceled the evening right then, but instead, I pushed through with my plans.

I opened the front door, motioning Griffin inside. His smile was wide. "Hey, Sammi. Thanks for agreeing to hang out with me tonight."

"It's..." Never mind. I was done trying to correct people in this town. It was a waste of energy. "No problem." I tugged on my boots. "Don't mention it." I meant that literally. I shifted my gaze toward the bedroom door. It was closed, but maybe he had supernatural hearing? Ugh. I couldn't even make it thirty minutes before acting like a loon again.

"You look nice."

I looked up and almost laughed. Sure, I looked real nice in Violet's oversized hoodie and flannel-lined jeans. Maybe if I was going to the lumberjack's ball.

"Thanks." Just because I found his comment hilarious didn't mean I had to insult him over it. I slipped on my coat and put on a hat. "Ready," I said, swiping a pair of heavier gloves. It was going to be a frosty one.

We went out into the biting air, and I pulled my coat more tightly around my neck. I wish I would've grabbed a scarf, but I wasn't about to go back inside in case I ended up calling everything off in order to appease my conscience. Going to the festival was still my best hope to discover a clue to Violet's whereabouts.

"You still want to go?" he asked. "We haven't even stepped off the curb and you're already shivering."

I rolled my eyes. "It's not like I moved to Southern California. Chicago gets just as cold, you know."

In actuality, you'd think I'd be used to this weather by now. I'd lived through brutal winters my entire life, but my body still hadn't adjusted. Luckily, it wasn't too long of a walk to get to the lakefront. Nothing was too long of a walk around here unless you ventured out into some of the swankier neighborhoods.

"I'm well aware where you moved to, Samm."

I wasn't sure what to say. I already felt mounds of guilt leaving Fernando behind, but now a fresh pile heaped over me reliving how I'd left Griffin without so much as a goodbye. He hadn't deserved that.

"I'm just not sure why," he said.

"How about we change the subject?"

He nodded and we walked a bit farther in silence. The snow crunching under our boots was enough chatter for me. It was a bit awkward hanging out with him again, knowing how I'd treated him, but at the same time, it felt like the most natural thing in the world—like I'd never left.

That was not a good sign. I didn't belong here anymore.

"Let's talk about this guy you're seeing."

"I'm not 'seeing' him. I told you it's more serious than that."

"Okay, so let's talk about this guy you're not seeing."

"That's not what…" I narrowed my eyes at him. "But if you must know, he's great."

We crossed the street and passed a group of cackling young teenagers. A pang of jealousy ricocheted through me. They had no idea how lucky they were to grow up as normal kids.

"That's it? Just great? I'd expect way more from you."

"Can we change the subject again?" *Boy, I'm going to be a fun one tonight.*

"All right then, Miss Difficult. How about *you* be the conversation starter and give someone else a chance to get knocked down."

He pursed his lips and stared straight ahead. Shoot. It was never my intention to irritate him. I glanced over again when we walked underneath a street light, and I detected the hint of a smile. He noticed me looking and it curved higher. Then he playfully shoved me.

"Come on, Sammi Pajami. Lighten up."

I giggled. *Giggled.* Wow, I hadn't heard that nickname in a while. I'd earned it in sixth grade after I'd mixed up my dates and came to school wearing pajamas, complete with bunny slippers, on formal day instead of pajama day. There was no part of me that hadn't flushed crimson, but Griffin and Sage cheered me on, convincing me I was a trendsetter.

"That's better," he said. "For someone who's supposed to be

78

happy, you haven't been acting like it."

"Who says I'm supposed to be happy?"

"You're not happy?"

Ack. "That's not what I meant. Of course, I'm happy. Happy with my life in Chicago. I have a lot going on there. Things are just a little... upside-down at the moment. I came here to see Violet, and for her own self-serving reasons, she made herself scarce. It's a long story, but I can't leave until I talk to her."

"I always have time for a long story." I shook my head. "Let me guess—another thing you don't want to talk about?"

"Yep." He opened his mouth but nothing came out. I could almost feel his thoughts bubbling out, though. There used to be a time when we talked about everything. Nothing was off-limits. Well, except for my witchy heritage. "When was the last time you saw my sister?"

He shrugged. "I don't know. A week ago, maybe. But I suppose you'll be leaving soon, now that you'll be talking to her tonight."

"Yeah, I heard all about her legendary hot chocolate. I'm really hoping she'll be there selling it, but something tells me she won't."

"Why? She's always—" My jaw dropped as I took in the sight before me, obviously making him pause and change course. "It's like you're seeing it for the first time."

I nodded. "It's so beautiful." I gaped at the entrance to the ice festival, already in awe and we hadn't even gone inside yet. "I'd forgotten how much."

"I can see that." He tugged on my arm. "So, what are we doing just standing here, then? Do you want to go in or admire it from afar?" He flashed me a smile, and I returned it.

"I want to go in."

It may be my only chance in Bigfoot Bay to have a nice, normal night.

CHAPTER SIX

$\mathcal{T}$he festival had only opened minutes before, but the place was already filling up. It was a preview of what was to come in a few months. It was the one event that would draw in hordes of both out-of-towners and locals alike for several weekends before settling back down in preparation of the busy summer season.

While we waited in line, I marveled at the icy arch we'd need to walk under in order to enter the park. Everything in the exhibit was carved out of ice, from the castles to the tunnels to the large slide at the end. Mind-blowing didn't even begin to cover it. Despite my less-than-thrilled attitude being back in my hometown, I was really happy to be here for reopening day. Chicago had a lot to offer, but Bigfoot Bay Ice Festival wasn't one of them.

"It's a shame this isn't open longer," I said.

"Agreed. Although, you'd probably change your mind if you were stuck inside a melting castle in the spring."

"Agreed."

The last time I was here, I'd also been with Griffin. We were just a couple of kids holding hands and loving life. It'd been so easy to get swept away amidst the snow sparkles and wintry palaces. It was magical without any magic involved... In other words, perfect. I had actually thought we'd be together forever. But what did anyone know about love at that age? It was crazy how silly teenage emotions could feel so serious once upon a time.

A hand waved in front of my face. "Sammi?" I noticed that we'd made it to the front of the line. "Where'd you drift off to just now?"

The purple and blue lights flickering off the ice tower ahead caught my eye, and I laughed and pointed in that direction. "I think I was hypnotized for a moment." I lowered my head to root around for some cash, but when I looked up, he'd already paid for two tickets. "Griffin, I can pay for myself."

"I know you can, but that doesn't mean you should. I invited you, remember?"

We stepped into yet another line to go through the archway. "This isn't a date."

He cocked an eyebrow. "I think we're both aware that you're not seeing someone who's too serious to see."

I chuckled. "Stop it."

"You're the one making this into a big deal, Sammi Pajami. Just relax and have fun."

He was right. Which only made me question my motives. I convinced myself that I'd accepted Griffin's offer for no other purpose than finding Violet, but I cringed at the thought of using him. But on the other hand, I especially didn't want to think of myself as someone who spent time with their ex just for the sake of spending time with them. The past was called the past for a reason.

The sooner I could leave Bigfoot Bay, the sooner I could put all my mental turmoil behind me.

"Thank you for the ticket." That was simple enough.

"You're welcome. I'll need to skip lunch for the next week or two, of course, but it was well worth it." He tapped his chin. "Or I suppose I could donate plasma again. That'll allow me from going hungry."

He attempted to hold a straight face but didn't succeed. I flashed him a dirty look which only made him crack up. He reached over and snagged a quarter from behind my ear and twirled it in front of me.

"Hey, look what I found," he said, pocketing the coin. "I can get a sixteenth of a cup of coffee with this. Thanks!"

Goofball. My eyes went from narrowed to rolling. "By the way, what are you doing now?" Since we were kids, I knew he wouldn't follow in his father's footsteps and go into police science, unlike his brother. That wasn't his thing. His thing was magic, as in tricks, not spells. "I always pictured you working as a magician, having your own show."

He opened his mouth, but the voice sounded behind me. Ventriloquist?

"Well, I'll be. Little Sammara Hain. Is that really you?"

I swiveled around to see the glowing face of Mrs. Fairchild. There were a few more lines etched in the corners of her eyes and a touch of gray sprouting from her hairline, but it was the same face I'd know anywhere. If I wouldn't, my mom would have my head, considering this was her best friend. She also ran the only hotel in town. Perfect.

"Mrs. Fairchild! How nice to see you again."

She came over and hugged me, then pulled back and took hold of my arms. "Just look at you, all grown up. You're even prettier than the pictures your mom shows me."

"Thank you." I squeezed her hands. "I'm so sorry about Mr. Fairchild. I didn't find out until it was too late and—"

She waved me off. "No worries. It was all very sudden. My

daughter's been helping out and keeping the vision alive. Besides, Edward's still with us in spirit."

"That's comforting to know."

I'd been so young when they'd opened Bigfoot Bay Hotel, the first one the town had ever seen, but I still remember all the flack they'd received. In the beginning, the community had objected, wanting to preserve the small-town charm, but Mr. and Mrs. Fairchild had persevered, and now it was one of our— I mean their—landmarks. It was a stunning, historic building with deep eaves and stained-glass walls, large enough to lodge a number of guests but small enough to maintain its quaint atmosphere.

Mrs. Fairchild brought her attention to Griffin a brief moment, and I swore her eyes twinkled. "Griffin," she said, "lovely to see you as well." He acknowledged her with a nod. "Why, it's just like old times seeing you kids together."

"No, it's not like that. We're just…"

She didn't appear to be listening because her focus was darting around me. "Is Violet with you too?"

My shoulders dropped. Even though I'd predicted it, I was still hoping I was wrong. "No. I take it she's not here?"

"Not yet, which is pretty unusual. We count on her every year, and she's always set up and ready to go in plenty of time before we open."

"And she's not staying at the hotel either?"

Her forehead furrowed. "Why would she be staying there? Is something wrong with her place—did a pipe burst or something?"

"Oh no. That's where I'm staying right now and it's perfectly fine. I'm just asking because I came into town to see her, but it seems like she's picked this time to go off on a mini-vacation somewhere."

"That doesn't sound like Violet. She wouldn't leave the shop, especially during the ice festival."

"That's why I thought she stayed somewhere right in town." I wasn't making much sense, but then none of this did. I was in good company.

"Unless she checked in under an alias and a disguise, she's not at my hotel."

Hmm. That was a possibility I hadn't thought of. If she could change a man into a frog, why couldn't she change herself into a whole different person?

But that still didn't explain what'd happened to Fernando's car. Unless she'd spelled that into a mouse, and it was sleeping peacefully under a woodpile right now. *Gah!* The endless possibilities and infinite outcomes were enough to turn me batty.

"Have you tried Bigfoot B&B?"

"The B&Bs aren't open this time of year."

"That's true for most of them, but Bigfoot B&B changed their availability a few years back." She waved and smiled at someone walking past. "They started opening for the ice festival weekends to accommodate the overflow from the hotel. We're always booked solid for this event."

"Great to know, thanks! I'll check with them."

"Not that she'd likely get a room when they're already so limited. And why would she spend the money anyway when she has a perfectly good place to stay? You know they charge astronomical prices."

"I'm just exploring all the options. She's gotta be around somewhere. As you said, she wouldn't miss the festival."

Mrs. Fairchild held up a finger to a woman behind the ticket table to indicate another second. "I need to get back and help out, but make sure you stop by and visit before you leave. Your mother would never forgive you if you didn't. And neither would I."

"Wouldn't dream of it, Mrs. Fairchild."

"Good." She patted my face lightly. "And if you're still adamant that Violet's on some kind of staycation, check with Helga Stein. She's around here somewhere. You can ask her if she's there."

"Will do. Thanks." Griffin and I walked away, and I whispered to him, "Mrs. Stein is still alive?"

He chuckled. "Surprised?"

"Yes and no." I thought she'd been over a hundred when I last saw the grumpy old woman who worked as a cook for Bigfoot B&B. "But I suppose eating all those little children must keep her young."

He busted a gut at my comment, and for a second I was ten again and we were daring each other to go into her kitchen. We were convinced the huge kettle she stirred contained all the kids who hadn't shown up for school. But then they'd return the next day, and we'd find out it was just a cold going around. However, that never stopped us from thinking it all over again the next time.

I transfixed on the castle in the near distance. It was my absolute favorite. It was a replica of Rapunzel's tower, and the entire thing was carved out of ice, all the way down to the long hair that spilled out the side, doubling as stairs. Once inside, there was a slide to get back down.

"Race you there," Griffin said, giving me a mischievous look.

My childish competitiveness took over, and I shot off without a word, getting a head start. I made it one step before him, but only because I slid on the slick ground, nearly colliding headfirst into the hard tower. I plopped to the crushed snow and rested a gloved hand on the sculpture.

"I win."

"Because I let you win."

"Did not."

"Did too."

Geez. What was the matter with us? A security guard standing near the attraction looked stern as he shook his head, pointing to the sign that read: *Anyone running or roughhousing will be frozen and sentenced to the tower for all eternity.*

What might've been a scary warning for a youngster caused a fit of giggles in a childlike adult. I mouthed *sorry,* which earned me a head nod and a twitch of his lips.

Griffin gestured to the stairs. "Milady."

I was about to climb up when a swarm of kids appeared, battling who'd be the first in line. "Um, this might not be the best time."

"Why don't we start at the end of the park and work our way back? It won't be as crowded."

"Great idea."

We bypassed all the shimmering ice sculptures and the families having the time of their lives. Some I thought I recognized, but so many visitors came in for the festival that I wasn't sure. But it was enough to trigger a bout of reflection, and that was not something I appreciated.

I wouldn't have given up Fernando for anything, but I couldn't help wondering what life would've been like if I'd stayed in Bigfoot Bay, like pretty much everyone else I'd grown up with. They were all here, raising a whole new generation, and I was the oddity who had left the beauty of this town before my prime. If magic hadn't existed, and I'd remained here, how would my life be unfolding right this very second?

For someone who claimed not to enjoy a stroll down memory lane, I was sure treading a well-worn path. I was acting like a crackpot, is what I was doing, and I needed to cut it out.

"How are your parents?" Griffin asked, cutting it out for me.

"They're loving Peru. It's right up their alley. Although, the phone service in their remote village is almost nonexistent, so I'm not able to talk to them very much."

"When are they coming back?"

"I'm not sure." In the meantime, they were renting out their house to a young couple with toddler twins and a brand-new baby. Sometimes I missed that house. *Sometimes.* "You know, Mrs. Fairchild didn't seem too worried about Violet."

"Should she be?"

"Not necessarily, but if my sister never misses the festival, and she's not home, where else could she be?"

Griffin stopped, causing me to halt as well. "Is there something more going on here? If anything's wrong, you know you can tell me. I'll do anything I can to help."

His voice was already tinged with worry, and I didn't want to amplify it. "No, we just had a fight is all and she's avoiding me. Hey, do you think someone in your family could track her down for me?"

"Because of a sisterly spat?" Now, his voice only held amusement. "That's probably not the best use of police resources."

Hmm. Maybe it was a pretty off-the-wall request. I knew I could receive assistance if I expressed a real danger, but I wasn't ready to cause a stir yet. And if I ever breathed a word about why I needed her back so desperately, it'd land me in the looney bin, and I'd never be able to help Fernando that way.

"Yeah, you're right. I'm sure she'll come around soon."

"If not, you might want to check Mrs. Stein's kettle. I dare you." He grinned and I gave him a playful whack. "Speaking of…" He pointed at a large, rounded lump. "Isn't that her?"

I peered closer, and the large, rounded lump was really a stout, knobbly woman hunched over. Her thick olive green and brown coat made her look like a moldy potato. She raised her head right then and glowered at me, causing an icy shiver to shoot up my spine. It was as if she'd read my mind, and I'd angered her.

"Yep, that's her all right," I said.

"Then why are you just standing here? Go and talk to her. Or are you scared?"

I scorched him yet another look and marched over, ignoring the heebie-jeebies crawling all over my skin.

"Hello, Mrs. Stein." My face held a smile, but I recoiled inside. The woman seriously creeped me out, especially because she hadn't stopped scowling at me. I was born into a family of witches, for Pete's sake; my palms should not have been this sweaty around someone who only played one in a Grimm's fairy tale.

"Been a long time, Sammara Eve Hain. Used to run from me like a devil was hot on your heels, now you're creepin' closer. What gives, girl?"

Griffin had sidled up beside me, but Mrs. Stein didn't acknowledge him. "Um, Violet. My—"

"You think I don't know Violet's your sister?" She grunted.

"Well, of course, but, um… I heard you're still working at Bigfoot B&B and—"

"She's not there."

"Oh. Okay." *Dang it, you creepy hag. Get out of my head.* The winter gust felt like a sauna compared to her presence. This was not a person I wanted to rile up. "Thanks for your time anyway. We'll let you get back to, uh, whatever it is you're doing." My tongue kept sticking to the roof of my mouth, like the dry air—or Mrs. Stein—had sucked all the moisture out of me.

"Have you seen Violet lately?" Griffin asked, and she swung her head toward him. Whew, it felt good to have her eyes off of me.

"Course I have," she spat.

"You have?" I perked up. "When?"

She scoffed. "For someone who just pops back into town, you sure are demanding."

"Mrs. Stein," Griffin said, "she's only eager to speak to her sister."

"Can't get a handle on your own family, next time don't be an outsider, eh?"

"Now, now. You know very well that Samm could never be an outsider. Once a resident of Bigfoot Bay, always a resident."

Man, could the woman grimace any harder? Her face couldn't afford to shrivel any more or it'd disappear within itself. I grabbed Griffin's arm. "It's okay. Sorry for bothering you, Mrs. Stein."

We'd only taken a couple of steps away before she called out, "Saw her this morning, sun was barely up."

I jerked around. "What? This morning?"

"That's what I said. You hard of hearing now?"

I pushed aside her nasty disposition; I was too stoked to finally have a lead, indicating she was nearby. At least I hoped so. Who knew where Mrs. Stein spent her early mornings? Well, besides hanging upside down in a bat cave.

"Where did you see her?"

"The bridge." She pointed a long, crooked nail toward the small footbridge at the edge of the park.

"What in the heck was she doing there?" Why would Violet be on a bridge next to the lake in the early freezing morning? She wasn't a troll; she wouldn't have been living under said bridge, so where was she staying? As far as I knew, she didn't hobnob with anyone who owned one of those multimillion-dollar homes right on the shoreline.

"What, I'm psychic now too? Could've been blabbering to the gulls for all I know. Looked out the window when making breakfast and saw her. Nothing more to it." She muttered, "Demanding child."

Geez Louise. "I appreciate the information, Mrs. Stein. Enjoy the festival." I pulled Griffin away while I sensed her glare digging into my back. "Wow," I whispered. "That was pleasant. It's a good thing she stays in the kitchen and doesn't have to interact with the guests."

"At least you know Violet's around here somewhere. You guys'll patch things up in no time."

"But isn't it a little strange that she was hanging around the bridge so early?"

He shrugged. "Maybe she was watching them set up for the ice festival." I brightened. Yeah, that actually made sense. I could practically feel my spirits lifting. "And who knows, she could've taken a nap and overslept because she was up so early, and that's why she's not here yet."

Yes, another rational explanation. She was still avoiding me, but she couldn't get away with that indefinitely. She had a life to live, just like I did.

"If she doesn't show up tonight, I know where I'm going at sunrise tomorrow."

I huddled my hands in the pocket of my coat. The gloves weren't holding up too well, but at least they weren't exposed like my face. The breeze had picked up and my nose was about to snap off.

"Do you want my coat?"

"Are you crazy?" I asked. "You can't walk around in only a sweater."

"Nah, I'll be fine. It's obvious you're freezing."

"I'll be fine too. I swear the temperature dropped twenty degrees since talking to Mrs. Stein. I think she hexed the weather or something."

"Or—and this may be a wacky idea, but hear me out—it could just be wintertime in Bigfoot Bay."

"Maybe," I grumbled.

He laughed. "It'll be much warmer in the tunnels. You still up for that or are you too old and stiff now to crawl through them?"

I elbowed him. "You're older than me, you know."

"By only six months, and if you remember, that used to be a sore spot for you."

"Funny how things change." When we were kids, it used to irk me to no end that he was older, and now, I was calling it to his attention. Perception was tricky like that.

"You need to talk to Violet that badly you'd come back here at 6:00 a.m.?"

"Yep. Not sure if she'll be on the bridge again, but it's worth a try."

"Need any company?"

"No, that's okay." When I did talk to her again, it would not be a conversation suitable for non-witchy ears. "Hey, check it out." I motioned to the ice tunnel, the last sculpture of the exhibit. "We lucked out. No line."

We went right over, and the attendant lifted a rope and waved us through. "First ones this weekend. Enjoy."

"How can that be?" Griffin asked him.

"It took a bit longer than the others to set up. You sure made it through the park quickly."

"We skipped to the end first," I said.

"Smart."

Griffin and I entered what had always been my second favorite of the festival. The tunnel's opening was high enough to walk upright at first, but if I recalled, that'd soon change. I hadn't grown more than an inch since my last visit, and I found I could still judge it correctly.

I ran my glove over the wall as we passed through, over the pulsing rainbow lights embedded in the ice. "This is incredible." More than a decade later and it still impressed me.

Griffin pointed where the tunnel narrowed before expanding into a small chamber. "Remember that?"

I unintentionally touched my lips then yanked my hand away the moment I realized. My cheeks blazed. Griffin was right—it was warmer in here. *Much* warmer.

"I wasn't talking about that, Sammi."

"Okay," was all I said, feeling like an imbecile. Again.

"I meant the carvings."

Of course, he was talking about the decorative carvings. What else would he have been referring to—our first kiss inside that room? Luckily for him, my sister hadn't found out or else he might've been speaking to me through a duck bill instead of lips.

We squeezed into single file until we were inside the area that had always reminded me of a prehistoric cave, complete with ancient symbols etched into the walls. It was the small details like this that made the exhibit so remarkable. Even looking at them now, I still couldn't decipher what they meant. When we were really young, we'd sometimes pretend to be archeologists on a mission to solve the mystery.

I heard the mumbling of people who'd just entered. "We'd better keep moving," I said. I'd already decided to make this the last stop of the night. I had to get back and rest up for the early morning. If all worked according to plan, there was even a chance I could return to the festival the following day holding Fernando's hand instead of his entire body.

We had to lower our heads to get out of the room and keep lowering them until we were crouched down. It'd only be a matter of time before we'd be crawling on all fours. The tunnels were wide enough to fit two adults side by side but stunted enough to warrant the huge warning sign that was posted by the entrance. Needless to say, it was not a feat for the claustrophobic.

"Is it just me or was this more fun when we were kids?"

We dropped to our knees—*oof!*—and shuffled along on the cold, hard ground. "Not just you," I said. Fortunately, the lights remained on throughout the entire thing so we weren't having to touch our way while plunged into darkness. "But definitely worth it." Toward the end, you passed through a section that made you feel like you were exploring the bottom of the lake. There was even a sea monster you had to climb over to get out.

"Definitely," he agreed. A flash of harsh orange light temporarily blinded us and we dropped our heads. "So, what'd you grow up to become—an archeologist or a marine biologist?"

"Neither. And I still haven't found out if you're making a fabulous living off your magic tricks."

"Sadly, no. I've barely done any magic in years. I kinda lost interest when my assistant left." He spoke it lightheartedly, but I still remained focused on the ground, even though the lights were no longer piercing my eyeballs. "I'm sorry, Samm. I didn't mean that the way it sounded. I wasn't dredging up the past."

"I know. It's okay. What is it you do then?"

"I'm a writer."

Whoa. That got my attention. I lifted my head and faced him. "A writer? You've got to be kidding."

He grinned. "Nope."

"The guy who barely passed English is now a writer?"

"Yep. Real books and everything."

Wow. "Books, huh? I don't recall seeing your name out there. What do you write?"

We rounded a corner as I waited for his answer. I could not wait to look him up. His books were going straight to the top of my to-be-read pile.

"Thrillers mostly. You haven't seen my name because I use a pen. I prefer to keep my anonymity, especially around here."

"I get that." Yeah, I could fully understand his need for

privacy, but by the same token, I fought the urge to invade it. I was dying to ask him what that pen name was. "I sure like me a good thriller every now and then. They're great when I need to stay up all night." *Hint, hint.*

We took a sharp turn, colliding shoulders. "Hmm. If I weren't mistaken, I'd say you were asking me to reveal my secret—"

My scream drowned out the rest of his words, or maybe it was the heavy clunking sound my head made when it whacked against the low ceiling as I sprung up. I didn't know, and I didn't care. Why should such trivial details matter when my childhood nemesis, Misty Evans, was right before me.

Frozen solid inside the tunnel wall.

CHAPTER SEVEN

"Tell me again what happened but slower this time." He dragged his hands down his face. "Much slower."

"Come on, man. Can't you see how shaken up she is? Give her a break. She's been through enough already."

I stared down at the steaming cup of coffee in my hand. I had to force myself to take a sip. It was extra dark and rich, the kind that makes your chest feel like a carpet. Under normal circumstances, I would've loved it. But now? Nope. This was about as far from normal as you could get, and ten gallons of joe wouldn't have been enough to drown out the ghastly image in my mind.

Misty inside the ice. *Frozen.* Her mouth wide open as if she'd been cut off mid-scream. Her hands pressed against the wall, fingers spread, giving the impression that she'd tried to claw her way out. Flippin' frozen stiff like some slab of beef in the butcher shop freezer. Ugh. Not a pretty sight by any means. I couldn't stand the woman, but even I wouldn't have wished her a fate like that.

I sighed, dropping my head. Griffin was right by my side

trying to comfort me. Trying to protect me from his older brother, a guy I'd known almost as long as Griff.

"Congratulations, by the way," I told Damon. "I don't think I've said that yet, have I?"

"See?" Griffin smacked his brother on the arm. "Now, she's delirious."

I waved it off. "No, I'm fine. Really." Well, as fine as I could be. "But seriously, your father must be so proud." I'd meant it sincerely in my brain, but when it had left my mouth, it'd come out sarcastically.

Damon humphed, and I wanted to assure him I was genuine. Since Griffin hadn't taken after his father in the law enforcement field like he'd hoped, at least one son had. Before long, Damon would be Chief of Police. If he could stay awake long enough.

"Are you happy?" I asked. "I mean, with the boredom? Being a cop in this town must be a snoozefest." I chuckled, the sound coming out garbled. "Of course, that doesn't apply tonight, right? But if you wanted more excitement, I'm sure you wouldn't have chosen something so gruesome…"

Great. Nothing was coming out as intended. I was babbling like a halfwit and probably hurting the situation more than helping.

I took another swallow of my coffee in order to shut my mouth up. Blech. It was cooling down too quickly. If there was anything worse than lukewarm coffee, it was tea, and since that was all Violet's shop contained, I'd have to suck it up and drink. Then again, what if all the caffeine caused me to stay up all night? I didn't want to just lie and stare at the ceiling, reliving the ice festival gone wrong. But if I did sleep, I'd likely have nightmares. I had to pick a lesser of two evils and stick with it.

"Can we please get back to the matter at hand?" Damon looked less than pleased; I was probably keeping him up way past his bedtime. I couldn't imagine there were many late nights spent crime-fighting in Bigfoot Bay.

"Sorry," I said, instructing my mouth to behave, "but there's not much more to say. Griffin and I went to the ice exhibit and were the first ones in the tunnel. We crawled through, turned a corner, and saw a Misty popsicle. That's it. I swear."

I drew out my words so slowly even a non-native English speaker could've understood them. I think that just annoyed him further. Dang it, I couldn't catch a break here. "Did I happen to mention how buff you look? You must've been hitting the gym pretty hard. Way to go." I initiated a fist bump but he didn't bite.

"What?"

I made a muscle. "You've bulked up. When you were a kid, you could've disappeared standing behind Sage." Seriously. Thirteen years earlier, I could've used him to knit a sweater.

"Do you think this is a joke, Samm?"

"What? Of course not. It's a compliment. And for the record, I go by Eve now." He'd probably need that information for his official report.

"I'm not talking about my physical appearance. I'm talking about your cavalier attitude toward finding the victim."

Maybe I was being too flippant, but I didn't know what else Damon wanted me to tell him. Cop or not, he was kinda being a jerk here. I knew he had a job to do, but after the rotten twenty-four hours I'd had, I didn't need anything else added to my garbage pile.

"You know, strike that last comment. I don't want to go on the record at all. I just want to go back to Chicago and..." Holy crud. Fernando.

"And what?"

I stole a glance at the closed bedroom door. Fortunately, Officer Beat a Dead Horse hadn't caught me looking. In all the craziness, I hadn't been able to check on Fernando yet. My head wilted. It was official: Worst. Fiancée. Ever.

"Are we done here?" Griffin paced the room, probably mistaking my head drop for a sign of exhaustion. "We did everything right. I called you the instant we found Misty, and we waited for you to arrive and investigate, even though it's brutal out there and poor Samm couldn't stop shivering."

"I was well aware of her discomfort, Griffin. Why do you think I gave her a ride back to the shop before I'd finished speaking with her?"

Oh yeah. Maybe I'd been too hasty with my jerk assessment. Damon hadn't kept me blue-lipped longer than necessary; he hadn't even hauled me down to the station. He allowed me to come back to familiar territory so I could dethaw with a hot beverage. Who knew the neighborhood gas station made such a decent brew? I filed that tidbit away for the next time I needed a fix at this hour. Wait, what was I talking about? I'd better not be around here long enough for a next time.

"You never did tell me what you're doing back in town."

"I came to visit my sister. I'm sure you saw the news in the local gazette."

"After all this time, what made you decide to come back right now?" I shrugged. "What's it been, about thirteen-fourteen years?"

"Thirteen. But who's counting."

"And where is your sister? I'd like to speak to her too."

"Good question."

Damon sat on the couch beside me, steepling his fingers. "You're saying you don't know?"

"That's exactly what I'm saying. I've been looking for her since I came into town, so if you see her, could you let me know, please?"

He stroked his stubbled jaw. "Interesting."

"Not to me. Look, I just want to see Violet then forget all this. My reunion home hasn't exactly been a celebration."

"Do you want to know what else I find interesting? You coming into the station last night during a blizzard and asking Officer Hansen to trace your fiancé's car. Care to tell me what that was all about?"

Griffin stopped pacing. "Fiancé?" I nodded. "Huh. I guess you were right about it being serious."

"Told you."

"Samm," Damon said, "why would your fiancé's car be in Bigfoot Bay?"

"I wasn't saying that it was. I only wondered if he could find it. As I'm sure Mike told you, he suggested a PI instead."

"Because you suspect he's cheating on you. You wanted to know if his car is parked in another woman's driveway." Officer Einstein thought he had it all figured out, did he? Ha. He was in for a surprise.

"And *this* is the man you're going to marry?" Griffin threw up his hands. "I knew he wasn't good enough for you."

I opened my mouth to correct him, but since Damon was listening in, what were my other options? I could say it wasn't a relationship concern, but then I'd have to come up with another reason why I was searching for his car. The situation was already messy enough. I sure hoped Fernando wasn't listening through the door.

"Cool your jets, Griffin. That's not the issue here."

Cool your jets? Was I talking to Damon or his father?

Griffin clenched his fists, and I took the opposite approach, melting into the couch and faking a yawn. "Can we be done now? I'm really tired." I rubbed my eyes for good measure.

"Not quite." Griffin threw up his hands again, and I appreciated his annoyance on my behalf. "Tell me about your fight with the victim that occurred earlier this morning."

My lids popped up. "My fight?"

"What the heck, Damon? She's not a suspect."

"This is the second time you called Misty a victim," I said. "Are you implying this was a murder?"

"I'm not implying anything. Victim is also the term I'd use for an accidental death." Damon's eyes never wavered from mine. "I answered your question, now answer mine. The fight?"

"Um, I wouldn't exactly call it a fight. More like a case of a demonic snake trying to eat my—"

I cut myself off with a gulp of nasty warm coffee, taking one for the team. I shuddered.

He tilted his head. "Trying to eat your what?"

I cradled the paper cup in my hands like it was a mug of the finest espresso. "Would you like me to run out and pick you up another one?" Griffin asked. "I can't imagine that's too hot anymore."

"That's sweet of you, but no. I'm fine. I'm hoping to be asleep soon anyway."

Damon didn't take the hint. "Trying to eat your what?" he repeated.

I frowned. "Trying to eat whatever was in my purse. That menace she carries around—sorry, *carried* around—should be illegal. Ask Mrs. Swanson at Murphy's Pet Store. She'll tell you the same thing."

"And that's what you were fighting about? Her snake?"

"We weren't 'fighting.'" I emphasized the point with air quotes, almost dumping the rest of the coffee on me. "I told you that already. She just got in my face in true Misty-fashion. I guess she wasn't pleased to see me again. It's no secret we've never been the best of friends."

"You have a pet?"

"Nope, no pets."

"Then why were you in a pet store?"

"Mrs. Swanson owns the place now, and she's always been my favorite teacher."

"If I recall—" All three of us directed our attention toward my dead ringing cell phone. "You gonna answer that?"

"Nope."

Damon stared it down like it contained all the evidence needed to crack the case wide open. Then he stared at me like I was hiding something. Whatever.

"What if it's Violet?"

"It's not."

The ringing stopped, just to start right back up again. "Mind if I take a look?"

"Be my guest." Damon picked it up and peered at the screen. "Let me guess. Unknown caller?"

Ignoring me, he hit Accept. "Hello." He pulled the phone away, scrunching up his face. Bringing it back, he said, "No, thank you. Yes, I'm sure. I said—" The voice echoing out the other end was high-pitched, but I couldn't make out the words. "Do I sound like someone who wants a subscription to Pink Poodles Weekly?"

He tossed the cell aside, and I chuckled. A haunted phone was amusing when it wasn't me on the receiving end.

"As I was saying," Damon continued, "Misty didn't get along too well with your sister either. In fact, there've been many public disagreements between them over the years."

"That I can't confirm or deny, seeing as I haven't been around."

"But you two must keep in contact with each other. Phone, email…" He glanced around. "Handwritten letters."

"My sister and I weren't pen pals. And she never kept me up to date on any so-called public disagreements with the… deceased."

"Hmm." He continued to scope out the place as if expecting

a lead to jump out from behind the soap bars. I understood him wanting answers, but he wasn't going to find them here. "I'd sure like to speak to your sister."

"That makes two of us—wait, are you implying *she's* a suspect?"

"Damon," Griffin warned but was met with a raised hand.

"Again, not implying anything. All I said was that I'd like to talk to her. I need to cover all my bases. I wouldn't be doing my job if I didn't speak with all the victim's enemies."

"Then you're going to be quite busy, chief-to-be, since you'll be needing to speak with the entire town."

He ran a palm over his face. "Mind if I check around a bit before I leave?"

"Don't you need a warrant for that?"

"Samm, I'm doing this for your protection. Considering the circumstances, I'd like to make sure everything's secure before I leave you alone."

My protection? I watched him poke around the shop as my mind raced after him. I still hadn't processed it all. He'd basically admitted that Misty's death was a murder without saying the words. Was it? Yes, she'd frozen in the ice, but how in the heck had she gotten inside it to begin with? Those sculptures weren't just made in the morning, and I'd seen her hours before. It was almost... supernatural.

Holy crud.

Could Violet have had a hand in this? She'd already proved she could do something despicable by turning Fernando soft and squishy, simply because she hated human males and didn't want one in the family. What was she capable of when it came to a fiendish girl she'd loathed all her life? Did my sister turn Misty into a freezy pop?

"Um, but weren't you the one who said it could be accidental? So, why do I need protection?" Damon peeked inside the storage closet. "It's not like someone could've easily stuffed her into a block of ice."

At least not by normal means.

He headed toward the bedroom, and my anxiety levels spiked. "At this point, I can't rule anything out."

"Well, did you speak with whoever owns the exhibit? It was their sculpture. And the attendant did say the tunnel took longer to get ready. Maybe there was a break in the wall and Misty fell in, and then..." And then what? That made as much sense as celebrating the Fourth of July in December.

"We're doing our job. Don't you worry about that." Damon stepped inside Violet's room. "I thought you said you don't have a pet," he called out.

"I don't."

"Does Violet?"

"Why do you ask?" I wondered if Fernando was hopping around, almost laughing at the thought of what his human form would do to Damon for calling him a pet. Griffin's brother may no longer have the physique of a string bean, but he still wouldn't stand a chance in that showdown.

My throat constricted. Comedy hour over. Unfortunately, Fernando wasn't in human form and had little defense against accidentally getting lodged underneath Damon's boot. I was starting to get up when he came out of the room.

"Because there's a bowl of water on the floor."

"Oh." Shoot. I'd forgotten about that. I waved it off. "That... that's for the fairies."

He raised an eyebrow. "The fairies."

"You know how eccentric Violet is." I rolled my eyes for extra effect.

Damon scrubbed his face again. Pretty soon he wouldn't have any skin left to scrub. "Everything checks out so I'll be taking off, but as soon as you talk to your sister, make sure she gives me a call."

"Will do."

"And make sure the door is locked behind us."

"Will do."

"One more thing." *Come on, buddy. Enough is enough.* "I'm not sure of your plans and how long you intended to stay in Bigfoot Bay, but I'd strongly advise you to stick around a while."

"What? Seriously? I have a life to get back to. What do I need to stick around for?"

"She has nothing to do with this, Damon."

"I'm not saying she does, but a woman was found dead hours after a very public altercation." Damon bore his eyes into me. "Just for my own peace of mind, what were you doing today between the hours of nine and six?"

"Well, I wasn't killing Misty, that's for sure!" This was absolutely ridiculous. I was being punished, that's what this was. See what happened when I left Fernando alone for too long? I stumbled into a murder investigation.

"Calm down, Samm."

"Shouldn't you be advising me to get a lawyer instead?"

He crossed his arms and sighed. I zeroed in on one of Violet's tea concoctions on the shelf; it wouldn't be the worst idea to choke down something relaxing. But I'd get far more stress relief conking Damon over the head with the glass jar instead.

He crouched down in front of me. "It'd make me feel a whole lot better to know where you were."

The look in his eye and the tone of his voice calmed me, making me realize he really was on my side. He wasn't out to get me. My overreaction was understandable, but I had to take it down a notch. I'd known the guy a long time, and he was doing me a favor by not forcing me to sit on a hard chair in a cold police station. I seemed to keep forgetting that.

"Okay," I said. "After the pet store, I came right back here and Sage visited and we caught up on old times."

"And you were with Sage until you left for the festival?"

"No, she left and then your brother stopped by."

He shifted his gaze to Griffin then back to me. "And then?"

Oh wait. I'd forgotten to mention about that woman—what was her name?—and Amy popping in. I frowned. Poor Amy. It wasn't her fault she shared genes with a demon.

"I was with Samm the entire time," Griffin said. "Now, give it a rest so she can get some sleep."

I whipped my head toward him, mouth gaping. I detected the slightest shake of his head before Damon noticed. At least I hoped before he noticed. Why would Griffin lie?

"Is that so?"

"Something wrong with that, Damon?"

They eyeballed each other while I drummed my fingers on my knee. I could've set things straight, but then I'd have to admit all those hours alone and unaccounted for. Hours that would've led right up to Misty's unnatural demise when I knew I had nothing to do with it.

"That's it, then," Damon said, digging his keys from his pocket. "Sorry to take up so much of your time, Samm. We'll be in touch. Remember what I said about Violet."

"Okay." After all that, it almost ended too easily. I couldn't wait for him to leave so I could speak with Griffin in private.

Damon grabbed hold of his brother's arm. "I suggest you leave with me, Bro."

Griffin paused a bit before nodding, but the quick look that passed between us was unmistakable. I knew we'd talk again soon.

I saw them out the door, triple-checked the lock, made sure

the shades were fully drawn, then made a beeline for the bedroom. I breathed a sigh of relief when I opened the door and saw Fernando sitting right there, blinking up at me with his cute little bloated eyes.

I scooped him up and held him close to my chest. Did frogs normally cuddle? I'd bet a no on that, but he was definitely snuggling against me. It went a long way toward easing my conscience. I was still figuring out how his amphibian brain processed information in relation to his human one, but I got the strong impression that he understood what'd happened and hadn't held the evening against me.

With him securely in my arms, I went over to Violet's phone and rang up Sage. It went straight to voice mail, which I'd expect at this hour.

"Hey, Sage. It's Eve. Or whatever you want to call me. I'm not sure if you've heard the news yet, but I need to see you tomorrow. Whenever you can fit me in. It's urgent." I glanced down at Fernando. "And please bring more blueberries."

"I swear we'll get this fixed soon," I cooed. I had no right to make such promises, but I vowed right then and there that I'd get the spell reversed before we had to walk down the aisle holding canes.

And there was only one surefire way to make sure that happened.

I had to find Violet before Damon did.

CHAPTER EIGHT

"*I*t was horrible," I said, knocking back a hearty chug of my virgin mango margarita. "Positively dreadful."

"You poor thing." Sage touched my hand. "I can't even imagine. I know she is—was—an awful person, but for you to have to find her that way…"

"I can't get the image out of my mind. It kept popping in all night."

So much so that I ended up sleeping through Violet's clock radio alarm, ruining my plans to go to the footbridge early. Not that I would've had access to it anyway if the area was taped off.

"If you would've seen her," I added. "Her face looked like one of your giant blueberries." I gestured to the bag on the table filled with juicy berries. "Thanks for bringing them, by the way." I held up the charger. "And this." It was thoughtful of her to remember that I'd asked for one. Maybe if I tried charging up my phone in the normal way, it'd stop the weird calls.

"Of course. Anytime."

I opened the bag and pulled out some blueberries. They

were gigantic, freaks of nature. I pointed behind her. "Is that our server?" When she turned her head, I slipped a few into my purse.

"Yep. Should I wave him over?"

"Yes, please. We could use some more chips." Sage and I were at Caliente, where she'd met me for lunch during her study break. We were stuffing ourselves with guacamole and sugar, mine in the form of syrupy margaritas and hers as multiple bottles of fizzy soda.

I folded up the bag. "How do you grow these things so big anyway? I've never seen anything like it."

"It's easy. I just ask them to grow big," she answered like it was the most logical thing in the world.

"Um, okay." Time for another drink. When the waiter approached our table, I ordered a second margarita to go with the chips, passionfruit this time. "And make it a double," I called out.

Sage laughed. "You do know virgin means without alcohol, right?"

"Doesn't hurt to pretend." As tempting as it was to anesthetize my current reality, I had to keep my wits about me.

"Are you making muffins or something?"

"Muffins?" I mumbled through a mouthful of salt-laden tortilla crumbs.

"With the blueberries. You asked for more after I just brought over a large bag yesterday."

I shook the remaining morsels from the bottom of the basket into my hand, then popped them into my mouth. That earned me a funny look. "What?" I asked.

"Maybe we should tell him to just leave the bag."

"Bite your tongue; there is no bag. You know they make them fresh here. That's why they're so delicious."

"Then we could wheel you into the kitchen and set you up next to the deep fryer. Save him a trip. Or ten."

"Ha-ha." I nodded toward her third soda, which likely meant it was her sixth of the day. "You have some unhealthy habits of your own, missy." I thought I liked sweets, but back in the day, Sage could pound the soda like nobody's business, and it appeared nothing had changed. How she could still get away with it without gaining an ounce or slipping into a diabetic coma was beyond me.

"It's only unhealthy if it doesn't agree with you." She stuffed a generous spoonful of guac into her mouth, and I wrinkled my nose. Sage didn't eat chips, only guacamole. It was like slurping down ketchup without the french fries. Who does that?

"Maybe unhealthy was the wrong word. I should've said peculiar. Very peculiar." In response, she stuck out her avocado-covered tongue. I was about to toss a balled-up used napkin at her but decided we were acting juvenile enough.

"You know what I think?" Sage said. "I think you're stuffing yourself with chips so you don't have to talk as much."

"But I am talking. Plenty."

"You're also holding something back."

"I already told you all about Misty and Damon's questioning afterward."

She eyed me through her glass. "There's more to it, I know it."

As if on cue, a brand-new supply of warm, crispy heaven appeared before me, and I dove right in. All right, maybe I *was* deflecting a bit, keeping my mouth full to avoid saying anything that would force her to run for the hills.

I stared at the purse in my lap. As badly as I wanted to, I couldn't tell her the truth.

"I *really* need to find Violet. Are you sure you can't think of anywhere else she'd go?"

"I'd be interested in hearing that answer too."

I jerked up to see Damon looming over the table. Lovely. I dropped my head to the side and rubbed my hand over my face, mouthing *no* to Sage.

She knitted her brows then smiled up at him. "Hello, Officer Kane."

"What are you ladies up to this afternoon?"

"Just a quick lunch before Sage gets back to hitting the books."

He pulled out a chair and plopped down. *Grr.* "Any idea where Violet is, Sage?"

"No, Officer Kane."

He turned toward me. "And you still haven't talked to her?"

"Nothing has changed since last night."

"And you're still planning on letting me know when it does?"

"Of course." Right after she unspelled my fiancé.

He rubbed his chin. "Care to tell me why you were buying insects yesterday when you don't have a pet?"

I nibbled my bottom lip. "They're a good source of protein. Did you know that?" Ugh. *Great answer, Eve.* I caught Sage making a weird face in my peripheral.

"Let me guess. They're for the fairies."

"Fairies don't eat bugs, Officer Kane." Sage slapped his hand. "Remind me to get them from you after lunch, Samm. And let me know how much I owe you."

"What?"

She narrowed her eyes. "The bugs," she hissed. "Geesh, have another margarita."

"She bought them for you?" Damon asked.

"Yep. They're for my greenhouse. Beneficial insects are crucial to the ecosystem."

My mouth gaped but I had no words. For all she knew, I had picked up a bag of black widows. What was going on here? First

Griffin, then Sage. I hadn't done anything wrong, but why were they covering for me? It was becoming convoluted.

"Since you appear to be an expert, would you happen to know if snakes eat those same beneficial insects?"

"You flatter me, Officer Kane, but I'm only knowledgeable about plants. I have no idea what snakes eat, although I'm pretty sure I once saw Misty feeding hers some maggot-infested steak. Probably left over from her breakfast."

He exhaled loudly. "And what about you, Samm?"

"Me? I'm hopeless around plants. I can't keep one green to save my life."

I swore he rolled his eyes. "Just tell me as soon as you have any contact with Violet." He stood and pushed in his chair. "Either of you."

"Yes, Officer Kane."

As soon as he was out of earshot, I said, "What's with all the formal 'Officer Kane' stuff? You've known him as long as I have."

She shrugged. "Just messing with him. It's fun. He's taking this so seriously."

"You don't think he should take it seriously? When was the last time there was a suspicious death in this town?"

"Yeah, but too bad it's one nobody cares about."

"Sage! That's terrible." Even if it was true, there was something inherently wrong about speaking it out loud.

"You weren't around her for the past thirteen years."

"Think about Amy." She raised an eyebrow, drumming her fingers on the table. "What? Okay, so maybe Amy won't fall into a deep pit of despair over this, but surely she cares at some level? Misty was her only family... Why do you keep looking at me like that?"

"Buying insects? Seriously?"

"Just a few crickets and mealworms. No biggie."

"Uh-huh. For protein, right? This must be some new Chicagoan foodie craze I've never heard of."

I stroked the zipper of my purse. "All right, if you must know... I'm taking care of a frog, and he's really important to me. He's... associated with Fernando. He loves your blueberries, by the way, and that's why I wanted more. It's the only thing he'll eat, so I'd really appreciate having as many as you can grow for me." Earlier that morning, I'd even gone back out to the market and picked up some leafy greens, strawberries, pepperoni slices. All were met with disinterest.

"Your fiancé loves my blueberries?" She swiveled her head around. "Is he here?"

"No, I was talking about the frog."

"Oh-kay. So, why is this some big secret around Damon?"

I massaged my forehead. "It's hard to explain. I just don't want it to be common knowledge that I have a frog." Yeah, that sounded sane. "Why did you tell Damon the bugs were for you? It's a good thing he didn't ask you to clarify which kind."

"Why? Because I know the history between you and Misty, and I didn't like how Damon was acting. Who cares what her serpent from Hell eats? We all had to deal with her enough when she was alive. Why put up with it in death too?"

I slumped back in my chair. "You should've seen him last night. But I get it. He's doing his job, and it's all fine now. At least with me. He's still very intent on finding Violet." *Get in line, mister.*

"Yeah, I bet."

"What does that mean?"

She rolled her eyes. "One thing that is *not* a big secret around here is how much Damon's in love with your sister."

"No way." She nodded. "For how long?"

"Oh, only for forever. It's so obvious too. I almost feel bad for the guy because it's not reciprocated. He couldn't get Violet to notice him if he wrapped his head in a tea bag and dunked it in her cup."

"Wow. I had no idea. But that aside, he's not just looking for her because of his feelings. He needs to cover his bases because of Misty and Violet's 'public disagreements' as Damon put it."

"He's right about that. There was a particularly nasty one not too long ago right inside the coffee shop. You could hear it from a block down."

"Do you know what the fight was about?"

"Not really. Misty was yakking away about something stolen from her. Violet threatened to stuff her in the freezer if she didn't shut up."

"What?!" The *freezer*? I nearly leaped across the table. "And you just thought to tell me this now?"

"Wait, you don't think she took off because she had something to do with this, do you? You said she was avoiding you because you were mad at her."

"I'm not putting anything past my sister at this point. Mrs. Stein told me she saw her yesterday morning on the footbridge near the lakefront."

"That old troll? I wouldn't take her word for it. I doubt her eyesight's too great."

"All I know is that I have to find Violet before the police department gets a hold of her. It's critical. If you hear anything about her whereabouts, tell me first, not them."

"Does this have something to do with that important frog of yours?"

My heart pounded wildly. "Why do you ask?"

Our lunch entrees—my enchiladas and her salad—hadn't even arrived yet and already I wanted it boxed up. My desire for food was long gone. Chips couldn't even tempt me anymore.

"You're sure acting weird."

"Sage, has anything not been weird since I came back?"

Her eyes flicked up as if mulling that over. "True."

"You'll keep an ear out then?"

"Yep. I can only imagine what would happen if Damon ever got her into an interrogation room. You might never see her again."

I'd worry more for Damon the Human. I wondered how he'd feel about spending the rest of his life as a cockroach. I couldn't imagine her taking too kindly to him professing his undying love.

"It still blows me away," I said. "Violet really has no idea that Damon's been pining away for her, yet the rest of the town knows?"

"Or else she turns a blind eye to it. Either way, I don't think you have to worry too much for Violet. Unrequited love or not, he cares too much to let anything happen to her."

"Enough to get away with murder? At the end of the day, he's still a cop."

"At the end of the day, he's also a man in love. Don't underestimate how much a Kane brother is willing to do for the woman he loves."

"Now, what is that supposed to mean?"

"Didn't you tell me Griffin covered for you last night? He told Damon he was with you the entire time."

"Yeah, so?" That reminded me. I had to ask Griff what was going through his head when he did that. Did he think I was guilty?

"I see it runs in the family," she mumbled, flagging down our waiter.

"I have no idea what you're rambling on about, but I've been confused enough lately without you adding to it." My head was like a kaleidoscope in a salad spinner.

"Never mind." We both asked for our lunch in a to-go bag since Sage was now running late. She slipped on her coat then reached for my hand. "As much as Misty provoked her, Violet could never do something like this. I don't know where your sister is, but she's innocent. I'm sure of it."

"Are you insinuating that I'm not?"

She laughed. "Of course not, silly."

It wasn't until Sage left when I realized how strange it was that it was never once mentioned how unusual Misty's death was.

And if this wasn't something Violet could ever do, who out there *would?*

I HUDDLED against the wall in the restaurant lobby and dumped half the blueberries into my purse. Having a frog wasn't unusual, but the same thing couldn't be said about carrying one around in a bag like a teacup poodle.

Fernando's skin was warm to the touch; the scarf was keeping him nice and toasty. Reassured, I zipped my purse back up and tucked it underneath my coat. Then with enchiladas and berries in hand, I took to the sidewalks, heading in a different direction. I had a sudden craving for a latte, and while I was at the coffee house, I might as well casually ask about the loud argument Sage had mentioned.

When I arrived at Bigfoot Café, I did a double take through the window. Griffin sat at a corner table with his back toward me, bent over his keyboard and typing furiously. Knowing that he was writing his secret books intrigued me more than it should have.

I took a couple steps forward while my attention remained on the mad typist, and *oof!* I collided into something unforgiving. In more ways than one.

"You idiot!"

"I am so sorry," I said, trying to place the woman's scarf-covered face when my gaze traveled to the brown snow. I wanted to smack my forehead. Her coffee was splattered all over the ground, courtesy of *moi*. I bent down to pick up the empty cup, but she elbowed me aside and snatched it herself.

"You need to watch where you're going," she hissed, attempting to scoop up the java slush. What the heck? Someone, please tell me she wasn't going to drink that.

"I know. I was being careless. Please, let me buy you another." Clouds of smoke billowed out of the cup. What in the world? "Just let me know what you're drinking." Was it coffee or fog machine juice?

"Don't worry about it." She stood, straightening her coat. "You've done enough already."

Wait, I remembered her now. And her name. "Clarisse, right? You came into Violet's Soap & Tea Emporium yesterday." More like trespassed. I should've recognized her snooty tone instantly. People like her rubbed me the wrong way. Just because she probably had a dozen servants at her beck and call didn't mean the entire world was bending over backwards to do her bidding and that regular rules didn't apply to her. I took a steadying breath. Despite all that, knocking into her *was* my fault. "I'm really sorry. Please, come inside. It won't take long. Let me get you another... whatever-it-is, and you can be on your way."

She smiled, flipping a one-eighty. "No, *I'm* sorry. For snapping at you. Nothing was done intentionally." She smoothed down her perfectly straight hair. "I've been on edge since, well, you know. The distasteful incident. Things like that just don't happen around here. I'm sure you understand."

Clarisse sauntered off with her dirty cup before I could respond. I knew it was Misty we were talking about, but "distasteful incident" sounded more like she was describing a plate of bad shrimp rather than a freakish death in Bigfoot Bay.

I shook it off and went into the café, only to notice the junior barista staring at me. She was probably wondering what had happened outside while I was wondering why she wasn't catching up on homework.

Griffin was still busy in the corner, earbud cords hanging down, lost in his own world. There was only one other person in the place, talking on the phone and eating a dinner plate-sized donut. Normally, during an ice festival weekend, the town would've been packed to the gills, but the huge boon to business hadn't occurred due to my grisly discovery the night before.

I stepped up to the counter. "Hi. I'll take a medium latte, please."

She nodded, pulling a cup from the stack and scribbling on it with marker. "Anything else?"

"Out of curiosity, what did the woman right before me order?" Baby Barista pointed to the sign that listed out the specials. The drink of the month was a smoky latte: A special blend of dry ice, espresso, and mocha syrup. Ah, no thanks. How was that even safe? "Just the latte, please."

She turned to start on my drink. "She's not someone I'd want on my bad side. I'd be careful if I were you."

"Oh, you're talking about that little thing outside? It was just an accident. It's all good."

She shrugged. "If you say so."

Not sure what she meant, but okay. "Hey, by chance were you working that day a bad argument broke out between Violet —she owns the shop on—"

She glanced over her shoulder. "I know who Violet is."

Of course. Silly me. "So, were you here when she and Misty Evans got into it?"

"Nope."

"Who was?"

She shrugged again. Well, that was helpful.

While she frothed the milk, I eyeballed the place. The click-clack of the keyboard echoed through the café, even drowning out the woman jabbering away on her phone. Griffin hadn't slowed his fingers once since I'd arrived. They were going to cramp up something fierce if he didn't let them rest. But then what did I know? I wasn't a typist. Or a writer.

I focused on what I did know as I studied the dessert case. The sweet symphony that arose from blending flour and sugar and butter was something I *could* understand, unlike the mental fatigue and carpal tunnel that surely would result from fast and furious typing sessions.

As I pondered my next foray as an amateur baker, I spied a chocolate chip banana loaf on the bottom shelf. I peered closer and chuckled. It looked exactly like Amy's "homemade" bread.

"Do you need a lid or will you be drinking it in the ladies' room?"

"No lid, and very funny." She set the cup on the counter, and I fished out a wad of singles from my pocket. "Keep the change."

I ignored her wisecracking snort and tiptoed over to Griffin's table. Not that it was likely he'd hear me approach, but I didn't want to rush over in a gust of air and alert him to my presence. I was too nosy, er, curious for that.

Ever so slightly, I glimpsed over his shoulder, hoping to catch a sentence or two. Some sleuth I was; my reflection prompted him to lower his laptop screen, but not before I caught a few words that made me blush. When he said he wrote thrillers, I hadn't taken him literally.

He swung around. "Sammi! To what do I owe the pleasure?"

"Um." I cleared my throat, no doubt growing redder by the

millisecond from my botched spying attempt. I had no business seeing what I just saw. "I, um, stopped in for a coffee and noticed you over here. I didn't mean to interrupt your flow or anything. You seemed really… focused."

"No worries. I could use the break. Take a seat."

I pulled up a chair. "Okay." I held up a bag. Oops, wrong one. I set the blueberries aside and showed him the one from Caliente instead. "Hungry? I have chicken enchiladas if you want them."

"I'm good but thanks." He took a sip off his coffee, keeping his eyes on me.

I gestured to his computer. "Is that a new book you're working on?"

"It is."

"What did you say your pen name was again?"

"I didn't."

Darn. I scrunched up my face, and he chuckled. "How do you expect to keep your writing a secret when you type in a public place?"

"Everyone knows I write; they just don't know what."

"But you know how everyone is around here. It'd be easy enough to peek over your shoulder and see."

"Like you did?"

His amused smile made me lean back and cross my arms. For a town that thrived on gossip, I hadn't been benefiting from it much since I'd arrived.

"It's not like I saw anything. Much." My cheeks rekindled, and his lips curved higher.

He finished his coffee, setting his cup at the edge of the table. "And how have you been holding up?"

"I'm sure the same as you. We were both there last night." It suddenly seemed wrong to complain about anything. At least I was walking around with a normal body temperature.

"I wasn't only referring to that."

"Then what else?"

"I can imagine how overwhelmed you must be. Coming back home to something like this, on top of dealing with your fiancé's unfaithfulness and—"

"Hold up." I raised my hand. "Is that why you told your brother you were with me during all my unaccounted-for hours? Because you felt *sorry* for me?"

"We both know you didn't have anything to do with Misty's death. Damon just needed to have it on record."

"You didn't answer my question. You're saying you felt bad for me? So, covering for me had nothing to do with you thinking I'm guilty?"

"Of course, I don't think you're guilty. Would you rather I did?"

Well, when he put it like *that*. I watched as the only other customer stood, slipping her phone into her pocket. Without her jibber-jabber, it was eerily silent in here.

"Need a refill?"

I jerked in my chair, the voice scaring the bejeebers out of me. The barista was standing near our table, smiling sweetly with a pot of steaming coffee in her hand.

Griffin waved his hand over his cup. "No thanks, Clare."

She went back to her post, and I whispered across the table. "She's a bit young to be the only one manning the place, don't you think?"

"If your sister can own her own store, I think Clare can handle managing a coffee shop."

"Yeah, but…" I stole a glance at her stacking up napkins. She might as well have been playing with paper dolls. "Violet is twenty-three."

"And so is Clare."

My eyes bugged out. "No way." Huh. Didn't anyone in

Bigfoot Bay age? "So anyway, about my fiancé... It's not what you think."

"If it's about him not being good enough for you, then it's exactly what I think."

"Griffin." My purse twitched in my lap, and I could sense Fernando getting restless. I rubbed the leather lovingly as if stroking him directly, silently assuring him that everything was okay and I was doing whatever I could to get us both out of this mess. "Trust me. He's more than good enough."

He steepled his fingers, tapping his bottom lip. I wanted so badly to explain, to fight harder for Fernando's honor, but I was already in a hole and worried about digging myself deeper.

"Talk to me, Samm. What's going on?"

"What do you mean?"

He sighed. "For one, you're rubbing your purse like you're expecting a genie to pop out."

I withdrew my hand. "It's exactly like you said—I'm overwhelmed, just not for the reasons you think. My sister's avoiding me, and I can't go home until I see her. Not to mention falling into a bizarre murder investigation within twenty-four hours of my arrival."

And *especially* not to mention the whole reason I returned to Bigfoot Bay to begin with. If Griff thought there was something off with me merely because I was rubbing my purse...

"We don't know that it was murder."

"Damon's not ruling it out."

"You really haven't talked to Violet yet?" I shook my head. "Aren't you worried? She's not one to leave her store for too long."

"As I said, we're fighting. She'll turn up eventually, but I really need to find her before your brother does. Would you be able to help me out with that too? I figured since you've already covered for me once..."

Uh-oh. Judging by his knitted brows, I'd pushed it too far.

"Did you know Damon has a thing for Violet?" I said, changing the subject.

He laughed. "Who didn't?"

Humph. Obviously not me until recently. "Don't you think that's a conflict of interest?"

"Samm, he's a cop with a serious case to solve. That's where his head's at right now. What, you think he wants to speak with her so he can ask her out on a date?"

Actually, they'd probably make a good couple. If he wasn't a lowly human male, that is.

"Yeah, I guess you're right." It was clear I wasn't going to get any more support from Griffin without raising suspicion. I'd have to take care of things on my own.

"You didn't sneak around the footbridge this morning, did you?"

"No, I overslept."

"Good. I'd feel better if you lie low for a while, especially when it's dark."

"I'm not on house arrest." I'd already decided to be at the bridge before dawn, taped off or not. I was determined not to slack off again, but it was best not to tell him that.

"I'm referring to your safety, and you know it. Whatever happened to Misty—"

"Might not have been a murder, is what you said."

"Exactly. It's still unknown. And until it's not, I want to know you're safe. Even if it turns out to be a fluke accident…" He gripped the table edge. "Where is this guy of yours anyway? In light of the circumstances, he should be here. Protecting you."

I rolled my eyes. "I don't need protecting. I'm fine." I was about to make a crack about the Middle Ages and damsels in distress but thought better of it. He looked really peeved. "Let's change the subject, okay?"

"Fine, as long as you promise you won't be wandering around a crime scene before the sun is barely up with the crazy hope of running into your sister."

"That's really specific. What about before the sun is up at all, does that work?"

I swore he growled. "Samm."

"Can you keep it down, please?" I whispered, spotting Clare's eagle eyes. She was dragging a rag over the counter, averting her stare the moment I'd noticed. I scooted my chair closer. "Whatever happened, happened to Misty," I said. "Yes, it was freaky and unexplainable, but it's not going to happen to anyone else. I guarantee it."

"And how exactly can you do that?" I dropped my head; I shouldn't have said that. "You know more than you're letting on, Samm. Why do you need to find Violet so badly?"

I wrung my hands. "Maybe because she's my sister. Maybe because she's the sole reason I even set foot in this wacko town again, and now she's gone and I can't even leave."

"It's not as bad here as you seem to think. It never was." His voice was soft.

I stood, clutching my purse strap in one hand and my two bags in the other. My latte remained untouched, minus one sip, on the table.

"If it's about me not belonging here, then it's exactly what I think."

I took off, storming past Clare, feeling both her and Griffin's eyes on my back as I slipped out the door. I was dead set on locating my sister, and I didn't care what I had to do to accomplish that before Damon and his comrades did the same. If she was linked to Misty's death, unless they had magical investigative techniques, they wouldn't be able to pin it on her anyway. But they could delay her, and I couldn't let that happen. I needed to wring that counterspell out of my darling sister and fast.

Fernando was counting on me. And sweet home Chicago was awaiting my return.

CHAPTER NINE

I smacked hard into a slab of cement and massaged my throbbing arm. Thankfully, my head still appeared intact. As my eyes acclimated to the surrounding darkness, an obnoxious sound snapped me into sitting position. I hadn't landed on cement, after all, but the bedroom floor. I'd fallen out of bed. Welcome back to my toddler days.

Another noise—*ring*—had me scrambling to stand. It was Violet's phone sounding from the other room. I caught the time as I ran out: 2:07 a.m. Who in the heck was calling at this hour?

I patted around, knocking something off the counter in the process. "Hello?" I grumbled.

"This Eve?"

"Eve?" I shook out a few more sleepy cobwebs. Eve... oh yeah. See what the place was doing to me? Only a couple short days and already I was forgetting my name. "Yes, this is Eve. Who's calling?"

"Sal. Your neighbor gave me the number." Fernando's brother. My spine straightened and my mind cleared, as much as it could for the middle of the night. "I need to talk to Nando."

Nando? Aww, cute. "Actually, I was hoping to talk to you, Sal. By chance, have you seen a—"

"I need to talk to Nando," he repeated with more impatience.

"Ah, he's not here." I glanced around the dim room, wondering if Fernando could hear me flat-out lying to his brother.

"You making excuses for him?"

"Excuses for what?"

"You in Bigfoot Bay?"

"Why do you think that?" Had Sal tracked me down? My throat tightened. I hadn't even told Mrs. Geller where I was. Did I have to worry about some deranged stalker showing up on Violet's doorstep on top of everything else?

"Your phone number." Oh. Blasted landline. If it were a cell, there wouldn't have been a blinking neon sign signaling my location. "He better not be hiding out there."

"Hey, I'm just here to see my sister. Speaking of—"

"Look, family or not, my patience is wearing thin. You see Nando, you tell him I want my money. Now."

My insides were strapped to a roller coaster. The nickname didn't sound so cute anymore. "Are you saying he owes you money?"

If he did, I hoped he borrowed it to buy an engagement ring.

"Yeah. And he can tack on another five for effing up my car. After what he pulled, that's the last time he's touching it. I ain't falling for any more sob stories."

The nausea intensified. Oh, Violet. What did you do? "What's wrong with—wait a minute." I flashed back to what Mrs. Geller had told me. "Fernando used your car?"

Which meant that Violet had taken off in Sal's car. Not good. At. All.

"If by used, you mean abandoned in the middle of a cornfield in Caledonia, buried in a snowbank, then yeah. He's lucky I have a tracking device, else I would've been really ticked off."

I gulped. He sounded angry enough already. The last thing I needed was for him to show up here and start poking around. "Maybe it was stolen? Someone could've taken it out for a joyride and..." I shut up, realizing I was hurting the situation. Of course, it'd been stolen. I didn't need to advertise it.

It didn't matter anyway because he ignored me.

"Do you know how hard it is to scrub wet grass off interior?" he said.

"Wet grass?"

"Whatever that mutt rolled in got everywhere. Stained it too."

"Stained?"

"Your idiot boyfriend's paying for this big-time. Unless you'd like to settle up on his behalf?"

"Settle up?" I flicked myself in the forehead. I was starting to sound like a confused parrot. "But I... I don't have any money. And he's not an idiot. He's your brother, and isn't family supposed to forgive?"

He snorted, and I almost did as well. I was one to talk about forgiving a sibling.

"Just tell him to step up and be a man, else I'm coming for him."

The line went dead. *Tell him to be a man.* Good one. If only it were that easy.

There was *no* way I was going back to sleep after this. I flipped on a light and began the prerequisite pacing. It was only a matter of hours before sunrise. At least there'd be no chance of oversleeping now.

Fernando was nowhere in sight. I didn't know if that indicated guilt or embarrassment. Or maybe it meant something else entirely. He could've been snoozing away, oblivious to everything.

So... I tapped my fingertips together. My fiancé owed money, and my sister had vandalized Sal's car. It was never Fernando's. I scanned my memory bank, trying to recall if he'd ever lied to me. I felt assured that he hadn't. He'd never claimed the car was his; I'd just assumed because he drove it. Other times, he'd come to my apartment on foot, which I never questioned because walking was a given downtown.

I stomped around as if the heavy pounding would reverberate up to my brain and snap the pieces into place faster. Ha! Joke's on me. If anything, it gave me a headache, making me more muddled than ever.

What information *did* I have to work with? For starters, there appeared to have been some weird grass incident that occurred either before or after Violet spelled Fernando. She then took off in Sal's car and drove to Caledonia. Given the size of the rural town, it shouldn't have proved too difficult to locate the field Sal had referred to. I strongly considered breaking Officer Damon's inane town-detention rule and traveling there myself. Then logic took over. It'd all happened days earlier and there'd been a blizzard to cover up any tracks. The farmland went on for miles. If there had been any evidence scattered about, Sal would've surely discovered it.

I let out a rush of air. The next question—how in the world had she left the cornfield? It wasn't like she could've hailed a nonexistent cab, and there were no bus or train stations in the vicinity. But somehow—hitching a ride?—she'd ended up back in Bigfoot Bay the morning of the festival and managed to take care of Misty before going into hiding again. It was enough to make me feel as if I were drowning in a teaspoon of water.

I returned to the bedroom and looked under the bed. After leaving the coffee house half a day earlier, I'd scoured Violet's shop from top to bottom, searching for anything that could shed some light. There was nothing out of the ordinary from what you'd expect to find in a soap/tea/stationery store.

The half-full cup shoved to the back of the shelf with murky leaves floating on top that resembled a tribal mask was a little weird, but considering Violet's witchy "talent" was reading tea leaves, even that wasn't too out of place.

The only thing I wasn't able to investigate sat underneath the bed. I dragged out the locked box again and shook it. I hadn't found a key on the premises and that drove me nuts. I was close to busting it open but hadn't sunk to that low yet. Violet was the impulsive one. I refused to stoop to her level by doing something she would do.

But then again… What was even the right thing in this situation? What if the box contained something that could help Fernando? No. I kicked it back under the bed. Unless Violet had shrunk herself and was hiding inside, I doubted anything in there would help. It was probably just filled with tax receipts and business stuff.

The only thing left to do now was wait.

The closer it got to dawn, the heavier my lids became. At one point, I had to hold them open, using my fingers as toothpicks. That settled it. If I had to stay here just one more morning, I was buying a coffeemaker.

When Fernando finally decided to show his little green face, I took that as my cue to pack him up and leave. The sun would rise soon enough anyway.

As I crunched softly over the snow-covered street, I did my best to ignore the peaceful air that blanketed me. Instead, I tried focusing on the sharp chill that stung my nose. For I knew the more I acknowledged the serenity, the more the town would draw me back in. I could feel it happening already, wrapping its gentle breeze around me, whispering sweet nothings in my ear. I tugged my hat farther down to stop the madness.

This was not my home any longer. I'd made that decision years before, and I was sticking to it. *Take that, Bigfoot Bay.* Pick another girl to woo because your charms aren't working on this one.

I neared the park; the ice sculptures were fenced off, but the footbridge was free. There wasn't a soul around and that was a bit of a letdown. I wasn't expecting a welcoming party, just one person who shared my DNA.

As the sun made its appearance over the horizon, I became gloomier. I'd put a lot of faith into what Mrs. Stein had told me, and I fooled myself into believing Violet would be on the bridge again. I stood alone, gazing out on the frozen lake, feeling as trapped as a fish caught beneath it.

"Oh, Fernando. What are we going to do now?"

What? I pivoted, my eyes widening. The trash can at the bottom of the footbridge was smoking. I swung my head around in a panic, searching for something to smother the fire. That had been my first impulse, until I'd realized I was overreacting and the entire town would not be engulfed in flames soon. It was only a dense fog. But a dense fog originating from a garbage can? I went over to check it out.

Tilted on its side was a paper cup from Bigfoot Café, piled atop the garbage. Steam swirled out of the top. It was one of those wacky drinks, and it was still active. How old was it anyway? I wasn't a dry ice expert, but I couldn't imagine the effects would last too long.

I hadn't noticed anyone around the area when I'd arrived, and I'd definitely been looking. The steam was now dissipating so quickly, I was convinced that whoever had tossed it out had just been here recently. Even with my somber mood clouding things up, it didn't seem possible that I'd miss them.

The B&B was a stone's throw away and there was light coming from the kitchen. If Mrs. Stein had seen Violet from her window, there was a good chance she'd also seen whoever was by the trash can.

I pushed aside my rapidly beating heart and crept toward the back door. But the more I tiptoed, the more I resembled a shady criminal. It wasn't wise on my part to sneak around after Misty's mishap. I imagined Mrs. Stein running out, iron skillet in hand, ready to clobber the figure slinking around the building at daybreak.

I straightened, making myself appear as harmless as possible, and walked right up to the kitchen door, rapping softly. I knew she was up preparing breakfast, unlike any off-season guest who'd be sleeping.

No answer. I tried again a bit louder. Then I sidled over to the window, only to immediately hurl backward into a heap of snow. At least I hadn't screamed; considering what had glared back at me, that was quite impressive. I looked up from my accidental snow angel into the angry face of a biddy interrupted.

I smiled through my shudder, giving her a little wave, and was rewarded with a deeper scowl. The face disappeared, and I pushed up and brushed myself off, wondering what I'd gotten myself into.

I peeked inside my purse to check how Fernando had fared the fall and saw a disgruntled frog. Then he ducked under the scarf. Hmm. That wasn't such a bad idea. If I left now, I'd be back at Violet's early enough to hide out under the covers for another couple hours.

What was I talking about? *Woman up, Samm.* I couldn't leave. This was too important. I smacked my forehead. *I mean Eve.*

"You pounding the screws back into your head?"

"What?"

Mrs. Stein eyed me through the cracked open door. "What're doing prowling around my kitchen this time of day, girl?"

"Um." My tongue stuck to the roof of my mouth. I needed to get a grip. There wasn't anything to be nervous about; I wasn't a little kid anymore. She was just a troll. Ugh. I jerked my head. I meant wizzled, old woman.

"You having a seizure or somethin'?"

"No, I'm fine. I'm sorry to bother you, Mrs. Stein, but did you see anyone on the footbridge this morning? Besides me, of course."

She stared at me like I had tarantula legs for eyelashes. "No." Then she tried shutting the door in my face.

"Wait!" I stuck out my foot. "Please. This is really important."

"Already said no."

"I have another question." She didn't respond, but at least she didn't stomp on my foot. "You told me at the ice festival that you saw Violet Friday morning around this same time. Are you positive it was her?"

She snorted. "You think anyone else around here looks like a walking cherry? Between her coat and that hair, girl's so bright it burns my eyeballs just talking about it."

I was familiar with the coat she spoke of, and it was... distinctive, but still. Owning a red coat wasn't that outlandish, but I wouldn't expect Mrs. Stein to appreciate anything other than shades of burlap.

"That's all you were going on—a coat? You didn't actually see *her*?"

She gave me a 'you're too stupid to live' look. "You're wasting my time. I was patient long enough, answering dumb questions, but these flapjacks ain't gonna flip themselves."

She closed the door before I could get a word out, followed by the window shades. I huffed. Well, that was that.

But instead of feeling deflated, my bubble expanded. It wasn't the most enlightening of conversations, but I'd made it through a one-on-one with Mrs. Stein and lived to tell the tale. I wasn't struggling to crawl out of her stew pot while she batted me down with a wooden spoon, so I took that as my good omen for the day, my kick in the pants. No more feeling sorry for myself. It was time to toss my tiny violin over the bridge.

Next up: ice sculptures.

I followed the fence line until I arrived near the back where the ice tunnel was. The area was not only fenced off but also had the customary yellow police tape circling it. I no longer had the benefit of darkness to conceal me, but I still had the morning hours of early March on my side. Unless it magically turned into a hot summer day, there wouldn't be anyone, save for a polar bear, venturing down to the lakefront to claim their spot.

After a quick inspection, I hopped the fence and crept to the tunnel. I was closer to the exit; I'd check there first. After that, I'd investigate the entrance. Misty had been found somewhere in the middle, and her body and the surrounding ice had been removed, but the rest of the tunnel remained intact. Even so, I wasn't brave or desperate enough to crawl through those parts just yet. Hopefully, it wouldn't even come to that. I could end up finding what I was searching for right away, even if I hadn't a clue what that was. I'd take anything that gave me a shred of hope.

Although, discovering a note stating Violet's whereabouts would be most appreciated.

I strolled around as if I were on a casual Sunday walk in the park, which I suppose I was. I just shouldn't have been doing it inside a blocked-off crime scene. I squatted down in front of the tunnel's exit and peered inside. A flash of color caught my eye several feet in, plastered against the wall. It was greenish and looked like a blade of grass. Yeah, the ground was covered in snow, but it still wasn't out of the ordinary to see a piece of grass pop up here and there. I was going to disregard it and walk around to the entrance when something told me to snatch it up.

I reached in and plucked it off the wall, bringing it closer for inspection. It wasn't grass but—

"What are you doing?"

I jerked back, stuffing the greenery in my pocket, pulse zooming like a chupacabra on a motorbike. Great. Just great. I slowly spun around.

"Hello, Officer Kane." Mike was also standing right outside the fence, but he looked much less uptight. Whereas, Damon's arms were about to snap off from him crossing them so tightly. "And good morning, Officer Hansen."

Mike fought back a smile. "Hi, Samm."

I nibbled on my lips, wondering how much trouble I was in. "Wow, you guys are stealthy. It's not nice to sneak up on someone before they've had their coffee." I clutched my chest for effect.

Damon sighed loudly, unnecessarily. His stance already told me I wouldn't be deemed Most Favorite Person that day. "Do you not understand what 'keep out' means?"

I raised my shoulders. "Yes?"

Damon dropped his head. "Samm."

"Yes?"

"Get out of there."

"Okay."

I ducked under the tape and vaulted back over the fence. If

they really wanted to keep people out, they should've made it more challenging. I wasn't exactly a track star, and I could easily hurdle it.

"Were you just about to go inside that ice tunnel?" Damon asked.

"What? No!"

"That's what it looked like to me."

"I was only investigating the outside. Honest."

"You don't think we're doing a good enough job?"

"It's not that." I held my purse as close to me as possible without making it obvious I was hiding something. Did he have the right to search it? "I just stopped by to see if anything triggered my memory so I could help you boys solve the case more quickly."

"If we need your help, we'll let you know. Until then, stay out of it."

"That's kind of hard to do when your entire life is wrapped up in the outcome." Damon cocked an eyebrow. It was a dramatic statement but true.

"It's not safe to be around the unmaintained sculptures. If any of these icicles would happen to break off while you're near them—"

"I understand," I said, cutting him off. "Perfectly." I gave them a big smile. "So, what are you two up to this morning?"

Mike's lips curved up, but surprise, surprise, Damon's expression was a tad grumpier.

"Samm."

"Yes?"

"Leave."

"Right."

I saluted him and walked back toward the street, my feet leading me straight in the direction of Bigfoot Café. I had a hankering for coffee with a side of information.

This time when I peered into the coffee house window, there were a good number of people inside. Once I was sure Griffin wasn't one of them, I went in. I was not in the mood to defend my expedition to the footbridge, and I knew he'd ask.

Clare wasn't behind the counter but instead a Zen-looking guy who appeared anything but at the moment. It was a shame that strands of his long, beautiful dreads would probably be pulled out before his shift was over. There was only one of him and a dozen impatient customers in line. Dang. It obviously wasn't the best time to ask questions and expect more than a frazzled grunt in response.

As I waited my turn—there was no way I was skipping the coffee—I planned my next errand. I'd tack a few chocolate muffins on to my order and then swing by Amy's. I didn't know what time she woke up, but at this rate, it'd probably be noon before I got out of here anyway.

Finally, I was at the head of the line and greeted with a sigh. "Yes, can I help you?"

I felt for the guy. If barista had been one of the many items listed on my resume, I would've jumped over the counter and given him a chance to catch his breath.

"A large dark roast, please." I pointed to the pastry case. "And three of those double chocolate muffins. To go."

His shoulders looked like a couple of elephants had been removed from them. "Thanks for not ordering the drink special. Those things are killer."

My heart sped up. "Killer?" My luck had turned. Was this man forking over an easy clue along with my bag of muffins? I tucked them alongside my purse after he'd handed them to me.

"Yeah, everyone wants one, and they take so freaking long to make. I can't wait till we stop serving them."

Oh right. They weren't literally a killer, of course. Did I think I was in a *Murder, She Wrote* episode?

He poured my effortless coffee and set the cup on the counter. "Everyone wants them, huh?" I asked.

"Yep." He rang me up as I took a sip. Delicious.

"So, if I asked you who ordered one bright and early this morning right when the café opened, what would you say?"

He handed me back my card. "I wouldn't say anything. I'd just laugh." Argh. That was what I figured. "Besides, I wasn't even here then. It was supposed to be my day off, but the person scheduled went home sick and I had to come in."

"Sorry to hear that." I stepped aside to let the next in line place her order. I'd already taken up too much of his time, but I had the feeling he'd welcomed the break. "Well, hang in there and have a nice day."

Silly thing to say. I almost rolled my eyes for him. I turned from the counter and heard, "Ooh... the smoky latte looks fun! I'll take three, please."

I glanced back and read the grimace through his smile. Poor guy. At least I'd done my part and made his morning a fraction easier.

I paused by the door and sipped my coffee while recalling the area. Once I was confident that I'd remembered the neighborhood where Amy lived, I was out the door with my purse secured warmly inside my coat. We had a short hike in front of us, and I debated about going back and getting my car. Nah, the exercise would do me good. I had a wedding dress to wear soon, right?

By the time I'd left downtown and walked the dozen-but-feeling-like-gazillion blocks, I was chilled to the bone and my remaining cold coffee wasn't doing me any favors. Why was I worried about squeezing into some slinky dress anyway? That wasn't me. Fernando loved me the way I was, curves and all. Unfortunately, I didn't hold the same attraction to him currently. *Sorry, honey.*

The doorbell was taped out of commission, so I raised my hand to knock. The door opened before my fist made contact. Good thing too; my toes were so stiff I could barely wiggle them.

"Samm? What a wonderful surprise! Come in, come in." Amy waved me inside. She was wrapped in a quilt, hair sticking up sideways. "I'm so embarrassed. I don't even have any hot coffee ready to offer you."

"Please, don't think twice about it. I'm fine. But what about you—did I wake you?"

"Oh no." She gestured me to the couch, and that was when I noticed the dark rings under her eyes. "You have to sleep to get woken up." She tried giving me one of her sunshiny smiles, but it fell flat.

I touched her hand. "I'm so sorry. Is there anything I can do?" She shook her head. I held up the bag. "I brought muffins."

"You're too kind, but I'm afraid I don't have much of an appetite yet."

"I understand." I set them on the table beside her. "I'll leave them here just in case it comes back later."

"Thank you."

She adjusted her quilt, tightening it around her shoulders, and I took that opportunity to glance around. The place needed circulation.

"Do you mind if I open up the blinds, let some light in here?"

"Oh, I'd rather you didn't. I don't need the neighbors peeking in and whispering about me."

Hmm, okay. I wondered if that happened often. It'd only been a couple of days, but I hoped Amy wasn't going loopy holed up in here. "Then how about I just crack a window or two? I'd be good to let in a little fresh air. I'll close them back up as soon as I leave."

"I suppose…"

I went over and raised the blinds just an inch to slide over a window to get some breeze inside but not enough to invite in the "Nosy Nellies."

"If only it were warmer out, I could open them more," I said, moving on to the next window. "We don't want you to freeze—" I cut myself off with a bite to the tongue. Horrible choice of words. "Uh, I didn't mean… Sorry. That was insensitive."

She actually chuckled a little. "Nonsense, Samm. It's fine."

Leave it to Amy to reassure me in her time of mourning. "Are you sure there's nothing I can do for you? When was the last time you drank something?"

"I had a sip of water this morning."

I put my hands to my hips. "One sip? You know that's not good enough, right? Maybe I should stay here a while and look after you."

"Don't be ridiculous. I have plenty of people who stop by and check on me. I'll be all right. I just need a little time, is all." I didn't want to rush her recovery, but I also didn't want her sitting around and wasting away if I could help it. "Actually, there is one thing… I could use some of Violet's calming tea. I know it'd help me sleep better."

Calming tea? Was that the same stuff Sage used? If it was, it was labeled as an herb I couldn't remember. "I'd love to help, but I'm not sure exactly what that is."

Amy tilted her head. "She's still not back?"

"Nope. Great time to take a vacation, huh?"

I tried to make it into a casual thing instead of the freak show that was really going through my head, but Amy wasn't buying it. She looked how I felt. "Where is she?"

"I'm not sure…"

"When will she be back?"

"I'm not sure about that either."

"How can you not be sure? She's your sister!"

She began to fidget, tugging on her hair. Wow, she really did need that calming tea. I didn't want to be the one responsible for a full-blown panic attack just because I didn't know my herbs. Maybe this was Amy's final straw, the rotten cherry on top of the curdled sundae she'd been buried in the past couple days.

I rested my hands on her shoulders and that seemed to relax her a bit. "We'll figure it out and you'll get your tea, okay? In the meantime, I'm going to get you a big glass of water, and I'm not leaving until you drink it all."

"Okay." She inhaled deeply. "Sorry about the little spectacle just now. I don't know what's gotten into me."

"There's absolutely nothing to apologize for."

"I know Misty could be an awful person, but she was all I had, you know?"

"I know." Amy didn't deserve any of this. Having Misty as a sister was enough of a life sentence; she shouldn't have to suffer through her death too. "Let me get you that water."

I went into the kitchen only to have my senses bombarded by overripe bananas. They were littered all over the counters, along with streaks of white powder that I hoped was flour. I pulled a glass from the cupboard, noting the open garbage can filled with burnt loaves. I didn't know whether to clean up or rent out the room as a science lab.

There wasn't a water dispenser so I filled up the glass with tap water, rinsing down some dried-up egg yolks glued to the sink. Other than her multiple failed baking attempts, there was no evidence that she'd used the kitchen for anything other than setting off the fire alarm.

Her cheeks were scarlet when I came back and handed her the water. "I forgot all about the mess in there. I wouldn't have let you go in otherwise."

I laughed. "I've been in Violet's bedroom. I'm no stranger to mess."

"I promise, I'm not usually such a slob."

"Don't worry about it, Amy. I'd be happy to clean it up for you, though."

"Oh no. I'll get to it soon. It'll be good for me."

I agreed with that. "So, baking's your thing?" I thought of the banana bread in Violet's fridge and wondered if she made anything else.

"I love it. I'm really good at it too, but I've been a little off my game lately... I thought it would be helpful to jump right back in—I'm one of the bakers for Bigfoot Café, you know—and I hate letting them down, but my heart's just not in it yet, I guess."

"Wow, I had no idea. I thought that chocolate chip banana bread in the case looked familiar."

"That's not all I make, but it is the most popular." Her face brightened as she spoke. "It was Misty's favorite as well, so maybe that's the reason I can't—shoo, now... go on, get!" She waved her hand frantically.

I followed my eyes down and almost keeled over. I had set my purse on the ground when I'd gone to get her water, and in hindsight, that could have cost me *everything*.

After that initial shock, I snatched up my purse and held it for dear life. Then I sprinted across the room and watched in horror as Misty's foul-headed snake slithered up my chair.

Amy reached over and plucked it from the cushion. "Good grief, Spike. Look at the ruckus you're causing. I am so sorry, Samm. He's not the cutest thing, but he means well."

Spike? I clutched my bag, silently thanking anyone who'd

listen that the zipper was closed. I peeked inside anyway to ease my nerves. With a name like Spike, who knew what the beast was capable of.

Amy let it free in another room and shut the door. "I thought I had him locked up, so I'm not sure how he escaped. Believe me, I wasn't gung-ho about adopting him, but I couldn't bring myself to get rid of him either. Misty would've wanted him to stay in the family."

I nodded, because really, what else could I do? My vocal cords were still paralyzed. And when the doorbell rang, I almost rocketed to the roof. Time to hightail it out of there.

I was closer to the door than Amy so I looked through the peephole. "Officer Hansen," I rasped, the feeling slowly returning to my throat.

"Mike?"

"If you're not up for a visit, I can tell him to come back later." I assumed he was there to talk about Misty.

"I got it!"

She practically flew past me, mimicking a lovestruck teenager on a first date rather than a sleep-deprived, dehydrated woman who hadn't faced the outside world in days. Huh.

Amy flung open the door, her face splitting in two. "Mike! How nice to see you!"

Were they an item? If not, it appeared Amy had herself a little crush. Good for her. If Mike could elicit this kind of reaction from her, she'd be back to her old self in no time.

"Good morning, Amy. How have you—Samm!" He plastered his attention on me. "I had no idea you were here. Twice in one day, and it's not even noon!" He chortled. "Long time, no see, eh?"

"Right." I smiled. "Well, I just came by to check on Amy."

"How thoughtful of you. I'm sure she really appreciates that."

"And now that I did, I'm going to get…" I darted my gaze between them, the urge strong to take off my coat. Even though the outside air was hitting me square in the face, it wasn't frigid enough to cool down the tension. Neither of them hid their emotions well. Amy was crossing her arms, the glower on her face so thick I could smear it across the floor, all because Mike's bouncing-off-the-walls grin was aimed solely in my direction.

He'd mentioned his adolescent crush on me that night at the station, and it didn't take Sherlock Holmes to figure out what her googly eyes meant. I did not want to drag Amy through any more heartache, so I had to make myself scarce before Officer Oblivious did any further damage.

"…going," I finished. Amy reversed her frown as if she hadn't been shooting daggers a second earlier. "Remember to let me know if you need anything at all, and I'll look around for that tea, okay?"

"Sounds wonderful, Samm. Thank you. We'll be in touch."

She gave me a squeeze, and I slipped out the door before her spirits came crashing back down. Either she was ecstatic to see me leave, or I'd imagined the entire thing. Since I tended to believe my eyes, the former was more likely. Ah, young love.

Because, you know, I was over the hill at the ripe old age of twenty-six.

I hunched over, keeping my head down as I picked up the pace down the sidewalk, trying to minimize the wind's sharp sting when it whipped into me. I hugged myself tightly, wishing I'd dressed warmer. *No, I take that back.* If I had a wish, it wouldn't be for warmer clothes. It'd be for Fernando's arms wrapped around me instead of my own.

Where was a fairy godmother when you needed one?

CHAPTER TEN

*B*y the time I made it back to the shop, I was chattering so hard I could barely fish the key out of my pocket. I stuck it in the lock, noticing the leaf stuck to it. Oh yeah. I'd forgotten I'd nabbed it from the tunnel.

Once inside, I began the process of dethawing. I'd just taken off my hat and coat when there was a knock at the door. I checked, seeing Sage's face peering back at me. After I let her in, I made sure the sign was still flipped to CLOSED.

"You really should keep the store open. You don't want Violet losing too much business."

"I'm not the one who told her to leave. And even if I were, I don't know the first thing about running this place. What if I mess something up and give someone the wrong herb or, um, bath soap? That could be dangerous."

Sage rolled her eyes. "Right, because we all know how deadly lavender bubbles can be."

I elbowed her playfully. "I'm serious. Earlier, I visited Amy and she asked for some calming tea. I had no idea what that was."

"It's the same tea you gave me."

"And I don't even remember that. See? I don't have a knack for this. I know the herb started with a C, but the only thing that comes to mind is coffee."

She shook her head. "It's chamomile and I'll show you. Just in case you don't have a knack for reading labels either." She smirked.

I narrowed my eyes and pointed to the bag in her hand. "If those are blueberries, I'll forgive you for insulting me."

She handed them over. "Yep. A couple pints. It's all I could get today."

Yes! I grabbed them. "It's plenty. Thank you so much."

"No problem." She glanced around. "So, when do I get to meet this berry-loving frog of yours?"

"Not all berries. He doesn't care for strawberries or raspberries or black—"

"Can I see him or not?"

"Well... maybe not yet. He's a little shy." She raised an eyebrow. "What is it with this tea anyway?" I asked, changing the subject. "I swear Amy almost freaked out when I told her Violet wasn't here and I didn't know what the stuff was."

"It's magical. Serenity in a cup. You should try it."

Magical? Sage didn't know the half of it. I bet Violet spelled everything in this place. Was that even ethical?

"I'll pass. I'm not really a tea person."

"You have no idea what you're missing. The particular species she sells grows around here so anyone can pick it, but your sister seems to be the only one who can harvest it at the exact right time. She gives it that special something you can't find anywhere else."

"Yeah, I bet."

She sighed. "I couldn't stop thinking about her last night. I'm starting to get worried. When did you get in that fight with her—three days ago?" I nodded. "This isn't like her, Samm. At all. She should've been back by now."

There was so much Sage didn't know about my family, and the secret was like an active geyser bubbling inside me. If I didn't get Violet back and everything fixed, I feared it would erupt and cause havoc.

"She's fine, trust me. I wish I could say more, but—"

"What if whatever happened to Misty could happen to her?" Her eyes widened. "Or already did?"

"You think she's trapped in a block of ice somewhere?"

"I don't know. I wasn't there to witness this epic fight of yours, but it couldn't have been *that* bad. Not enough for her to hide from you this long."

"Unless she's also hiding from the cops."

"Samm! This is your sister we're talking about."

Exactly. And I was the only one who knew what she was capable of. I whacked my forehead and held up a finger. "Excuse me a moment." I dashed into the bedroom with the bag of berries and let Fernando out. "Go nuts, big guy."

I shut the door behind me and returned to Sage as quickly as I could, not sticking around for his transformation from shocking pink to blueberry purple as he dove in.

"What was that all about?" she asked.

"Do you trust me?"

"Of course."

"About Violet... Remember at lunch you said you're sure she's innocent? Well, I feel just as strongly that she's not in any danger. Except from me once I find her," I muttered. "I even have a lead."

"Really?"

"Do you happen to know if she knows anyone in Caledonia?"

149

"Caledonia? That's a strange question. And no, I have no idea."

"Okay." It was worth a try. "How about you show me that tea now?"

She scrunched up her face. "Why do you think she's in Caledonia, of all places?"

"Just a hunch." We scanned the jars with C names, finding the right stuff, albeit running low. I waved my hand. "Let's see if there's another jar in the closet."

"You're acting bizarre again."

"It's this town, I tell you." I went into the storage room and tugged on the light cord. "Chamomile, chamomile..." *Ah, here it is.* I plucked it from the top shelf.

"That's not chamomile."

"That's what the lid says. Or is this another crack about me not being proficient in reading labels."

"No..." She flattened her lips and peered closely. "It looks just like it, but it's not." She scrutinized a few jars, touching the glass as if reading braille. She pulled one down labeled chicaweed and said, "Here. This is chamomile."

"What?" I took the jar from her. "That's not what it says."

She shrugged. "That's what it is."

"How can you tell?" I studied both jars and the dried leaves looked almost identical. Also, I couldn't be sure until I matched them up, but they also resembled the—

"Because it told me."

I gave my head a sharp shake. "Wait, what?"

"The chamomile told me what it was."

"Um, okay." I thrust the chamomile-labeled jar into her hand. "This is chicaweed, then?"

"That'd make sense, but I have no idea."

"But I thought they talked to you?" I said, only half kidding.

"Only the local plants. This one is out of my jurisdiction."

All right, then. I left the closet. Sure, a plant-whispering best friend sounded off the wall, but if I thought about it, much less so than a family of witches. One of whom turned men into frogs.

I grabbed the leaf that I'd confiscated from the crime scene and inspected the trace of gold running up the underside. "Is this chamomile?"

Sage walked over, and I placed it in her hand. She rubbed it against her palm. "No."

"Then I'm guessing it's this other herb since they look the same." Maybe Sage's confidence in Violet's innocence was unwarranted. "What do you know about chicaweed?"

"Nothing, I'm afraid. I've never heard of it." She held up the leaf. "Where did you get this?"

"It was by the ice sculptures," I said casually. "Something told me to take it."

She glared at me. "You should not be going over there. You're going to get in trouble."

"Can I use your phone to look this up? Violet's still in the dark ages here." Didn't she realize how much easier her life would be, and how much more normal, if she just broke down and bought a computer like the majority of the rest of the world?

"I forgot it at home. What about yours?"

"It's dead."

"I gave you a charger. Did you forget to use it?"

"Nope. See for yourself." I gestured toward my cell plugged into the wall. "Charging since yesterday and still dead as a doorknob." Her charger had done nothing so far, but it wouldn't hurt to give it another day and see if something took. "It's not your charger that's the problem. It's my phone."

Sage frowned, going over to look. It picked that time to ring.

Did I mention my haunted cell phone also had a sense of humor?

She gave me a look as if to say *Dead, huh?*

I smiled in response. "Go ahead. Answer it. It'll be fun."

She took the bait. "Hello?... Wait, hold on, please." She extended the phone toward me. "You won some tickets to a bridal show. Do you want them?" Her look was smug, falsely thinking it was a perfectly normal call.

"Ask where it is."

I hadn't entered any bridal-related contests. I'd only gotten engaged four days earlier, and I'd been a tad busy since then.

"Where is the show located?" Sage asked. She made a face, and I chuckled. "That's not a real place... No, it's not. Unless you mean Seattle?... Um, Washington... The United States... North *America*... You know what, never mind. We'll have to pass. Thank you anyway." She set the phone down. "It's in Emerald City."

"Yeah, I figured it was something like that."

She retrieved the phone and flipped it over. After messing with it a bit, she frowned. "The phone's dead."

"I know. That's what I've been telling you."

"But..." She glanced back and forth between me and the screen, shaking her head.

"Too bad the show isn't around here. I wouldn't mind checking one out." If for no other reason than to sample cake.

"I'm sure they're a dime a dozen in Chicago. Speaking of, how's it going with Griffin?"

"Don't you mean Fernando?"

"No, I think I know the difference."

"Apparently not, since we're talking about bridal shows and I only have one fiancé."

She plopped down on the couch and inspected her fingernails. "He never got over you, you realize. Not after you left and took his heart with you. I'm referring to Griffin here, in case you were confused."

"I know who you're talking about." I rolled my eyes. "And we were just kids then."

"Doesn't matter. He never forgot you. Not even during that year he was engaged and—"

"He was engaged?" I blurted out. My stomach did a little flip. It made zero sense. "To who?" I searched my memory for any woman around our age who he'd be compatible with. Nope. Not a single one came to mind.

"She's no one you know, and be thankful for that. Moved here several years ago and already left. I think she put a foul taste in the town's mouth, and it spit her out."

"Why didn't they get married?"

"Not sure. He doesn't talk about it."

"But I don't get it. If she was so bad, why would Griffin even be with her in the first place?"

"I dunno. You'd have to ask him that." She laughed. "Maybe she cast a spell on him."

My gut twisted further. I knew Sage was only speaking in jest, but what if it was true? How could I assume there weren't any other witches in the surrounding area? It was ignorant to think we were the only ones. Griffin was a terrific guy, and I couldn't imagine him getting involved with an unsavory woman unless he wasn't in his right mind.

That'd be like him marrying Misty. Blech. Oops, I mean, may she rest in peace.

"Why does your face resemble the guacamole we ate yesterday?"

"I think I just need some air." I fanned my face. "It's kind of stuffy in here, wouldn't you agree?"

"No."

"Well, it is."

I paced the room while Sage snickered. Yeah, I was a freaking barrel of sea monkeys. I flicked her a look of annoyance, and she responded by laughing harder. My return home had been one glorious revelation after another. What was next?

"Samm. You can't blame Griffin for moving on. Or at least trying to. In case you forgot, that's exactly what you did."

"Of course, I don't blame him."

"Then why are you upset?"

"I'm not upset." To prove my point, I stopped patrolling the grounds. "I'm… it's complicated." I twisted a purple strand around my finger as she watched me through a corkscrew curl that flopped down her forehead.

"Do you remember when we were eight and you found that stray dog?" she asked. "You convinced your parents to keep her as long as you put up lost dog notices and contacted the shelter. They said you could have her as long as no one else claimed her within a week. You were so excited when it got to six days and you were sure the dog was yours."

"I remember, but what has it got to do with anything?"

"Because when I told you Griffin had been engaged, you had the same look as when the owner showed up to claim his dog."

"You're crazy."

"Am I?" Her lips twitched. Well, wasn't she just the little cat with all the cream? Whatever. She stood and gave me a quick peck on the cheek. "Gotta run. Call you later."

The moment Sage left, my cell phone rang again. I ignored it. I didn't need magazine subscriptions or pizza pies or an Oz wedding or whatever else was coming through the line. The ringing stopped, only to resume while I was comparing the leaf I'd found to the ones in the chicaweed jar. The tone was higher this time as if someone had cranked up the volume.

All right. Geez. It was like a defective smoke detector. I marched over, ready to stomp on it when I noticed the screen was flashing *Mom*.

What I wanted to know—why was she the only "real" person to get through on this phone?

"Mom?"

"Oh, Samm." She sounded relieved. "I'm so glad I reached you. Any word on your sister?"

"Not yet."

"That's what I was afraid of."

"Where are you?" My guess was still out of the country since the line was choppier than the bangs I'd given myself in first grade.

"Your father's been working on getting us a flight home early. It's not easy, well, with the monkeys and all."

Um, okay. "Why are you leaving early? Is your research done?"

"How can you even ask that? We need to get back for Violet."

"Violet's fine, Mom. I told you we had a falling-out and she's been staying away until it blows over. I'm still in Bigfoot Bay like I promised, so I'll be here when she returns. You don't need to rush home." I debated telling her about Misty, but then she'd for sure rush home. On Pegasus, if needed.

"Sammara Eve Hain!" I pulled the phone from my ear when a bunch of screeching static came through. Either that or she was hissing out expletives. "Just because you refuse to listen to the signs doesn't mean the rest of the family is as stubborn. There's been foul play. I can feel it."

"Foul play?"

"Fortunately, I also feel your sister's unscathed—*for now*—but something's not right, and if you're not going to get to the bottom of it, someone has to."

Why couldn't I have been talking to my father instead? "I'm working on it," I muttered. The old-fashioned way, creeping around crime scenes and asking questions. Not by gazing into teacups and reading cloud shapes.

"Whatever's going on isn't your fault, but it is your responsibility. Remember that, Samm."

"Oh, I'm going to find her. You can count on it." I pulled the charger from the phone and went into the storage closet. "Since I have you on the line, do you know anything about an herb called chicaweed?" While I waited for her reply, I switched the lids on the two jars.

"Of course. That's the whole reason we're in Peru. They call it the marvel leaf."

"Really?" I perked up. I knew it! Violet was involved in this somehow.

"Yes, why are you asking?"

I scoured her herbal stock, wondering what other secrets the room contained as I grasped at straws just out of my reach. "I don't know…" There was an empty spot where a jar used to sit before it fell and broke. That happened right after… "Clarisse!" I blurted out. I'd completely forgotten that she'd wandered in here. Could that snobby gold digger be in cahoots with my sister? Or… I shuddered.

"Clarisse?" my mom said.

"Yes, Mr. Jones's widow. What do you know about her? Is she a witch?"

"A witch? Good heavens, no. You'd know that too if—"

"Let's not get into that now. What about Clarisse and Violet —are they close?"

"What do you mean by 'close'?"

"Friends, Mom. Are they friends?"

The ideas were spinning fast and furious. Did Clarisse sneak into the shop the other day to swipe some chicaweed for Violet, who then used it to ice Misty? Was that the "special" order she wanted? I needed to take a deep breath and think it through. Just because I found a nonlocal herb in the tunnel didn't mean it was used as an ingredient in a freezing spell.

"They hardly have much in common. Seriously, Samm."

"She stopped in a couple of days ago to pick up an order."

"Nothing unusual about that. Clarisse suffers from horrendous migraines and gets feverfew from the shop. It's the only thing that helps her cope. My opinion? She doesn't belong here, and the town is letting her know it. If she just left, so would her headaches."

What was it with people thinking Bigfoot Bay was alive or something? The town didn't care who lived here or not. Wait, did she say feverfew? I was almost positive that was the jar that broke. So, maybe that was the herb she stole, and I was back to square one.

"What can you tell me about this marvel leaf? Is it used in spells?"

"Almost anything can be used in a spell, dear. You'd know that if—"

I sighed. "Okay, Mom. I get it."

"Then you shouldn't ask questions you don't want the answer to. And while we're on the subject, you'd better take extra care since you insist on not protecting yourself properly. It's a good thing your sister had the common sense to hang mugwort over the door or else things could've been much worse."

No need to mention that I took it all down the other day. I'd gotten fed up with spitting out a mouthful of the nasty-tasting stuff every time I walked in.

"Bigfoot Bay is safe. I don't think I have to worry about—"

The line went dead.

It took me a whole half of a second to decide what to do

next. I ran into the bedroom and scooped up a very fat and happy Fernando who'd consumed the entire two pints of blueberries. I put him in my purse, threw on my winter gear, and was out the door, sprinting to the public library. I made it there in minutes. Fortunately, Mrs. Booker, the warmhearted, gray-bunned head librarian, remembered me since my card expired ten years back. Unfortunately, they closed early on Sundays. I didn't have much time. She handed me the password and a key to one of the private computer rooms, and I dove right in.

It felt like I'd entered a sweatbox; I had to peel off half my clothes before I could even begin. If I just allowed myself to back down and get another phone, I wouldn't be dealing with this right now, but to do so was akin to throwing in the towel. I was determined not to be here long enough to need a new one. I'd take care of that task when I was home in Chicago.

I logged in and searched for chicaweed. Immediately, a picture popped up of a healthy plant with small, fuzzy yellow flowers. I clicked around further and found a dried version. The leaf showed the same golden stripe underneath as the one I'd found.

A medicinal herb found in the Amazon rainforest. Native to Peru. Already knew. *Locals call it the marvel leaf due to its almost-supernatural abilities to successfully treat everything from minor skin conditions to depression to late-stage cancer.* Knew that too, partly. *Scientific name: Banax veriditas. Takes five years to mature. Grows low to the ground. The active constituents isolated...* Blah, blah, blah.

I quickly skimmed through data that would've excited Sage to no end. It wasn't as if I didn't appreciate the wonderment of the so-called miracle plant, but all the technical jargon made my head swim. It was not my thing. I just wanted to get to the good stuff, but what was I expecting to find? *A Spellcaster's Guide to Chicaweed?* Funny how I was actively seeking out magical information when only days before, I wouldn't have touched it with a ten-foot broomstick.

I came across something that read like a medical journal, itemizing all the curative properties when used in low doses but becoming toxic in higher quantities. A classic case of "the dose makes the poison."

Nothing at all about freezing someone to death. Imagine that.

The knock almost sprung me from my chair. Mrs. Booker cracked open the door and pointed at the clock. Already?

There's always tomorrow, I thought as I prepared to leave. But just before I'd X'ed out, a small block of text caught my eye: *Adverse effects intensified by significant levels of carbon dioxide. Local folklore describes instances of combining the leaves with the Cavena fern to induce a catatonic state.*

Catatonic state? Throw in some ice and Misty Evans came to mind. While that was the most engrossing thing I'd read so far on chicaweed, it left me more confused than ever.

And I couldn't escape the feeling that Clarisse was somehow involved. Maybe she and Violet were nothing more than acquaintances. Maybe her wandering into the supply closet was only a case of needing her migraine remedy. Maybe she wasn't working with my sister or connected with Misty's death in any way.

But maybe she was. And if that was true, Violet could be hiding out in her mansion. The possibility wasn't that far-fetched. Clarisse could've even picked her up after she'd ditched the car in Caledonia. It was the most rational explanation I had so far.

I left the library and headed back to the shop to get my car. I had to talk to Clarisse and get to the bottom of this, and she lived much too far to walk.

I rounded the corner and spied someone leaning against the

front door. A man. But not just any man. He turned his head and stared straight at me. I blew out a puff of air. There was no avoiding him now.

"Care to explain what you were doing this morning at 6:00 a.m.?"

Oh crud.

CHAPTER ELEVEN

"*H*ello to you too, Griffin."

"Samm…"

"I get it. You're not very happy with me right now." That was an understatement. His expression would put Grumpy to shame. I should've known Officer Blabbermouth would tell his brother. Like it was any of his concern. We weren't a couple anymore.

"I asked you not to go there. It's too dangerous."

"Yes, but if you think back, I never agreed to it."

He groaned. "What are you doing?" I thought it was pretty clear. I was using my coat sleeve to brush snow off my windshield. I gave him a look, stating the obvious. "I know *what* you're doing, but why are you doing it? Where're you going?"

"There's something I need to do." I should've fired back with, *Why were you engaged to a woman not good enough for you?*

"And what is that?"

I dug out my car keys. "For a private person, you sure are inquisitive about others. You don't like to divulge anything about yourself, yet you want to know everything about everyone else? Hardly seems fair."

His jaw dropped. "What are you talking about?"

Ugh. What *was* I talking about? I wasn't acting normal, that much I knew. "Sorry, don't mind me. I guess I'm not myself right now." He grabbed the keys from my hand. "Hey!"

"Wherever you're going, I'll drive."

"No, you won't."

"You just admitted you're not yourself."

"So?"

"So, that means you're not driving. Get in."

I almost told him that I'd changed my mind, but I really did want to get this over with sooner rather than later. And it wasn't the worst idea to have him along for backup, in case Violet wasn't there and Clarisse tried anything underhanded. There were at least twenty rooms she could've locked me in before anyone would even know I was missing.

"Fine," I said.

Griffin opened the passenger side door, and I slid in. When he got behind the wheel, he tipped his imaginary cap. "Where to, boss?"

"Very funny. I'm going to the late Mr. Jones's house."

"What?"

"That monstrosity of a mansion on the outskirts of town."

"I know where he lived."

"Then why are you looking at me like I have three eyes, and they're all crossed?"

"Why in the world do you want to go there?"

"To see Clarisse Jones. She, uh, came into the shop asking about a special order."

"What's going on, Samm?"

"I just told you. Now, are you going to drive me or not?"

He responded by shaking his head, but in an 'I don't get it' way rather than a refusal, since he'd pulled out of the spot and was driving in the mansion's direction. I zoned out the window, taking some much-needed time to work out my plan. I had no clue what I was going to say when I confronted Clarisse, but I was more interested in her houseguest register. Maybe I could get Griffin to distract her while I snuck in.

I used the blissful silence to my advantage, mentally scanning over the information I'd discovered at the library. Something about the carbon dioxide thing hounded me. I wasn't a plant expert, but even I knew the basics.

"Plants take in carbon dioxide, right?"

"Yeah…" Griffin glanced at me, furrowing his brow. "Are we playing trivia now? I didn't prepare."

Adverse effects from excess carbon dioxide were a given with people; could it also hurt plants? Maybe it altered their structure or something.

"Can plants get too much of it? Like, 'too much of a good thing is a bad thing'?"

"I don't know. Probably. Why are you even asking this?"

"I'm not sure. I'll let you know when I am."

He just shook his head again and continued driving. It wasn't long after that when we arrived at the gated manor. To my surprise, the fortress wasn't on lockdown. Very fortunate since that was one hurdle I hadn't even considered. This was one fence I wouldn't be able to leap, and it looked much too hostile to climb. What with the medieval-looking spikes sticking out of it and everything.

"You sure you want to do this?"

"Yep. Drive on up. There's a reason the gates are open."

He inched in slowly, not questioning me. I just hoped that reason wasn't to lure in unsuspecting victims as food for her pet hellhounds. The jitters increased the closer we approached, but the second he parked, I squashed those nerves and jumped out like I belonged there. Griffin turned off the car, catching up to me by the lavish fountain.

I attempted to peek in a window, but Griffin pulled me back. "What do you think you're doing?" Before I could answer him, the front door opened and I darted back. I never even had to ring the bell.

"Can I help you?" the woman asked, obviously a servant based on her uniform. I bet Clarisse had at least an army of them working for her.

"Yes. Can I speak with Clarisse, please? She's expecting me."

I'd mapped it all out at the last moment. I was going to talk about her herbal medicine, ensuring that I'd get an order put in for her as soon as possible. Once I engaged her in conversation, I'd figure the rest out along the way.

"I'm sorry. Mrs. Jones is resting. She's been ill and needs to stay in bed."

Hmm. Some plan. I'd just been sent on a detour. "But I just saw her at the coffee house…" When was that? My days were starting to run together. "…yesterday. She was fine."

She tsked. "I told her to stop drinking those things, but does she listen? No, she does not. And now look at her."

"Stop drinking what things?"

"That wretched smoking coffee. It can't be good for her, but she continues to get them. She's addicted. Perhaps after they kill her, she'll finally listen to me."

"Right. Well, can I speak with Violet then?"

"Who?"

"Violet Hain. The woman staying here with flaming red hair? You really can't miss her."

"There are no guests here."

"You sure? Maybe I could just check around a bit. I promise

I won't get in the—*eek!* What was that for?" I asked Griffin who'd just yanked my arm.

The servant lady began shutting the door. "I must get back to work now. Please leave."

"But—"

"We're going," Griffin said, more to me than to her. He dragged me to the car and opened my door. "What is wrong with you?"

"You're the one pulling me along like that invisible dragon you used to have. Remember that thing? You had this cool leash—"

"Samm, *what is going on?*" Geez. I was a little fed up with getting interrupted all the time. "Why were you asking for Violet?"

"Because I'm looking for her. You already knew that."

"And you think she's here, of all places?"

I shrugged. "Worth a shot."

After I buckled in, he darted around to the driver's side as if I were a flight risk. He backed out, keeping his eyes on me the entire time. And he had the gall to lecture *me* about safety.

We were several blocks out when it clicked. *Boom.*

I faced him. "Griffin, you have to turn around and go back."

"What? Why?"

I wasn't even sure myself, but it all fit together somehow. I'd stake my life on it. Unfortunately, all I had were a bunch of unassembled pieces and couldn't see the whole picture. But I'd get there.

"Dry ice is just solid carbon dioxide, right?"

"Trivia again?"

"Just tell me I'm right! And you're not turning around."

"You're right, and no, I'm not. I think you need to lie down."

"You don't understand. I bumped into Clarisse at Bigfoot

Café yesterday and knocked the drink out of her hand. It was one of those dry ice specials, and she was really upset at first."

"Okay. And?"

"And guess what I found smashed against the ice tunnel wall? This out-of-place rainforest leaf that apparently is affected by significant levels of carbon dioxide. Don't you see? Misty's death had something to do with Clarisse! I bet her servant was lying. She's probably not even sick at all."

I was afraid he'd get whiplash from how hard he jerked his head toward me. "Hold on a minute." He swung into the spot in front of Violet's store. Ugh. I guess he wasn't turning the car around. "First off, we are not going back. Second, what in the frick are you talking about?"

He had a point. It was better to gather more evidence first. I had to return to the tunnel. Maybe there'd be another clue. My brain was ping-ponging all over my head. It was possible that Violet was only hiding from me, after all. Her lying-lowness could have nothing to do with Misty. As unnatural as her death was, could it have been the result of an exotic herb and the Bigfoot Café monthly special?

"Samm." He touched my arm, making me flinch. "I know you're under a lot of stress right now with all your domestic issues and—"

"Domestic issues? What the heck, Griff?"

"I was trying to say it nicely."

"Once and for all, Fernando is not cheating on me," I said through gritted teeth.

"Okay, okay. It's not my goal to rile you up and make you feel worse."

I hung my head. Now, he was just placating me, and I did not appreciate it. Why did I even care if he believed me about Fernando? The important thing was that I knew the truth.

"Can we just get back to the matter at hand?" I said. "One

of the things troubling me about Clarisse is motive. You've been around—did she have anything against Misty?" He looked dumbfounded. "All right, I know. Stupid question. *Everyone* had something against Misty."

"Are you even listening to yourself?"

"Of course, I am."

"I'm going to give you the best advice I can right now. Go inside and get a good night's sleep."

"It's two o'clock. In the afternoon."

"Can't hurt to get a head start."

I slapped my thighs. "You're absolutely right. I'll go do that. Thanks for the words of wisdom."

My hand gripped the door handle, ready to bust out when he held me back. "Don't even think about it, Samm."

"Think about what? Oh right"—I snatched the keys from the ignition—"thanks for reminding me not to leave without them."

"That's not what I meant, and you know it. Do not get involved in the investigation."

"Aren't I already?"

"I mean it. No more amateur detective work. Leave that to the professionals. If you found something you think is important, let my brother know, but don't go running around accusing people."

I kept mum. I'd said too much already in the adrenaline rush of the moment. And since my mind still flip-flopped back and forth regarding Violet's involvement, it was best not to tip anyone off to her whereabouts before I got my hands around her neck.

Let Griffin think I was a stressed-out, delusional woman scorned. I could deal with that for now.

"Thanks for your concern, Griffin. I promise I won't do anything dangerous."

"You already did by going back to the ice sculptures. There's no one taking care of them and making sure they're safe to be around."

"Yep. Damon already filled me in. I'll talk to you later, okay?"

I opened the car door and had one foot on the ground when he stopped me again. For someone who thought I needed rest, he had a funny way of showing it.

"Listen, there's a possibility that Misty's death was a result of negligence. I'm not playing around when I say the sculptures aren't safe. Stay away, Samm."

I turned toward him. "Negligence?"

"If the festival reopened prematurely, the company could be held liable. If the exhibit wasn't sufficiently frozen, the ice could've melted down in such a way as to break off and cause an accident. I don't want the same thing happening to you."

My eyes widened. "That's... ridiculous. It sounds like you're saying a falling icicle killed Misty."

"It can't be ruled out."

"She was encased in ice. That must've been some icicle." Geez. If he wanted to keep me away, he'd have to do better than that.

I slipped my other foot out, gave him a little wave, then hightailed it out of there before I burst out laughing. I didn't want to disrespect his concern for me, but come on... an *icicle*?

My teeth were still clamped to the insides of my cheeks when I entered the shop. I didn't think he was flat-out lying so much as exaggerating the heck out of the situation, but in a way, it was kind of sweet.

In a 'childhood guy friend I knew since I could finger paint' manner of speaking.

I peeked out the window to see him still sitting in my car. Hmm. At least he didn't have the keys. I tossed them on the corner table and opened my purse, letting Fernando leap out. As soon as Griffin left, I would take a casual stroll to the lakefront, but until then, I might as well make the best of it.

"It's just you and me now, sweetie. Let's spend some quality—"

Croak! He hopped off to the bedroom as if I weren't even there. He seemed to cop an attitude whenever I spent time with Griffin, but couldn't he understand that jealousy was the least of his issues? I wasn't doing anything wrong; on the contrary, I was busting my hump so he could get his ribs back.

"Fine," I grumbled. "Be that way."

Another five minutes passed, and Griffin was still there. Then ten. Then fifteen. If he was planning on sticking around a while, he was going to get mighty cold without the keys to turn on the heat.

I opened a bag of chips to temper my hunger pangs while I waited. It was only a matter of time before he left, and it was still early. I could hold out longer than him. He was dressed as if it were a warm spring day in the type of weather where you could build a snowman out of your breath.

The next time I checked, I almost choked on a chip.

CHAPTER TWELVE

"*A*re you freaking kidding me?"

A Bigfoot Bay police car was parked beside mine. Griffin was leaning out the driver's side window, chatting with Mike. Then I watched Griffin walk away while Officer Hansen stayed.

I waited for Mike to get out of his car and come to the door, but he just kicked back in his seat like he was on a stakeout.

A stakeout. And I was the stake-e.

"Are you freaking kidding me?" I said again, not that anyone was paying attention.

I stomped outside, Mike lowering his window as I got closer. "Hello, Samm. Beautiful day, isn't it? Wow, third time seeing each other in eight hours." He chuckled. "In some countries, that'd make us married."

Ha-ha. Hilarious. "Can I help you with something?"

"Oh no. I'm pretty comfortable already, but thanks for the offer."

"Then do you mind telling me what you're doing here?"

"Official police business." He tapped his badge, and I rolled my eyes.

Police business, my freezing fanny. I marched my coatless body back inside and slammed the door. Obviously, he was there because Griffin had asked him to spy on me like some common criminal. What a lovely use of the town's resources. Didn't he have garden gnomes to rescue?

Griffin's charming concern had turned into metal bars. I had no doubt that Mike would follow me if I left. Was it that big of a deal to keep me away from the ice sculptures? I was being treated like a child here. It was enough to make me throw a tantrum.

I dialed Griffin's number and got voice mail, leaving a few choice words before hanging up. One perk of an old-fashioned phone rarely enjoyed anymore: Slamming it down. It was satisfying and oddly relaxing.

After letting off some steam, I occupied my time by organizing Violet's stationery. First by color, then by time period, followed by occasion. If anyone came in asking for rose-colored Victorian tea party invites, I'd be ready.

I ate another small bag of chips, an apple, drank a bottle of iced mocha. Paced around a while. Planned out my schedule when I got out of lockdown. Nearly rocketed to the ceiling when a vase shattered to the floor. I groaned. Fernando had jumped on the shelf, knocking it down, and wedged inside a teacup in the process, the one with the weird leaf pattern floating in it. I should've rinsed it out days ago, but that was Violet's business, not mine.

Once I'd freed him from the cup and rinsed him off, I set about cleaning up his mess while he hopped back into the bedroom without so much as a bleep of gratitude or beg-pardon. I grumbled to myself as I swept broken glass into the dustpan.

What did frogs and human men have in common? Apparently, neither were capable of admitting they were wrong.

When I'd finished clearing the floor of sharp shards, I checked on the scene outside. The sun was retiring for the night. I wished I could say the same for Mike.

Unlike Griffin, he *did* have access to a heated car, but how long could he sit there without taking care of basic needs? I didn't even want to think about what these guys had to resort to. I could hardly see how I was worth the trouble. Or was there something I didn't know about?

It didn't matter; I was going stir-crazy. Maybe Mike was keeping himself comfortable by not drinking or eating anything, but there'd eventually come a point when he'd have to do that too. It gave me an idea.

I rang up Sage. "I'm looking for an herb that makes you sleepy."

"Yeah, I can imagine how everything must be catching up with you. You should really try Violet's calming tea."

"I want more than calm. I want comatose. And it's not for me."

"You want to drug someone?"

"No." But after the way she put it, it did sound pretty bad. And illegal. "I'm looking for a peaceful little lullaby, an aid to rock someone into a deep sleep just long enough for me to slip out."

"You're not making sense. Are you in danger?"

"No, but Griffin is convinced I am. He has Officer Guard Dog camped out in front of the shop so I don't sneak off. But I'm so close, I can feel it. I'm sure I can locate Violet if I just tie up a few more loose ends."

"This is about Violet?"

"Indirectly, but yes."

"Well, why didn't you say so in the first place? I'll take care of it."

"You will?"

"Sure. Hang tight and I'll be there in a bit."

She hung up. I nibbled on my bottom lip, wondering what she was up to. After another hour passed, I was about to call her back when there was a knock on the door.

I opened it to Sage's beaming face, holding up a steaming paper cup. "Thought you could use this."

"Um, thanks?" I accepted the large coffee, waiting for her to elaborate.

"I gave Officer Hansen one too. I was just popping over to bring you one since the café accidentally made me an extra, and I saw him sitting there. I told him he looked like he could use a little pick-me-up, so I offered him mine because he told me he's on official police business. It's my civic duty and pleasure to help out a fine officer from the Bigfoot Bay Police Department."

"Okay."

"Don't worry. Yours has caffeine. Lots of it." I popped off my lid and peered inside. "Unfortunately for Mike, I can't say the same for his. His caffeine somehow got replaced with tincture of Skull Root."

"Skull Root?" The lightbulb just sparked on. I'd only asked her to point me toward a sleep aid; I never expected her to take care of the deed all on her own. "It sounds... ominous. It's not going to hurt him, is it?"

"Nah. It sounds much worse than it is. It's actually harmless. Tasteless too." She winked. "Gotta go. Good luck."

"Wait! Aren't you worried you're going to get in trouble for this?"

She waved her hand. "If anything, I'm doing him a favor. He's going to wake up feeling more refreshed than he has in years." She paused a moment. "I'm not exactly sure what's going on with you, but I trust you have good reasons and you'll tell me soon enough. And you'll bring Violet back. So, it seems I'm following a higher purpose here." She blew me a kiss and floated off into the night.

Wow. Did I have loyal friends or what? Not many people out there would knock out a cop for you.

I settled in on the couch with my coffee, opening the blinds just enough to give me a clear view of Mike. He'd parked close enough to a street light (that for reasons unbeknownst to me wasn't always functioning) but as luck would have it, the bulb was burning bright that night and I could see inside the car with ease. There was no reason on his part to remain hidden. I was being stalked legally.

As I sipped my coffee, my lids drooped lower while Mike appeared bright-eyed and bushy-tailed. I had a rush of panic. What if Sage had inadvertently switched the cups? *Deep breath.* Who knew how long the stuff took to work? I was probably freaking out for nothing, but I dumped the rest of mine out just to be on the safe side.

I returned to the couch in time to see the cup at his mouth. Whether it was his first sip or last, I wasn't sure. I kept my eyes glued to him as he fiddled around on his phone.

The next thing I recalled, it was 5:00 a.m. Jiminy Cricket. I vaulted up, convinced I'd been Skull Rooted, even if I felt the opposite of refreshed.

The one saving grace was Mike snoozing away, but who knew for how long? I had to get out of there while it was still dark. I poured a full bottle of water down my parched throat and changed clothes. What I needed was a quick shower, but I'd already wasted almost a third of my day watching the back of my eyelids.

"Fernando?" I called out. "Come on, we have to go."

I searched around, eventually finding him under the bed

behind the locked box. I lay down and stretched out my arm, but it didn't reach that far. Grrr....

"I'm sorry, okay? You can be mad at me later." He blinked but didn't budge an inch. I knew how hard it was on him, my spending time with my ex, and I'd probably acted too harshly when he'd plowed into the vase, but this whole twisted situation hadn't exactly been a basket of Caliente's homemade tortilla chips for me either.

I dragged out the box, then left and returned with a broom, sliding it underneath the bed. All he did was hop over it as I moved it back and forth like it was a game to him.

"I get it. You're the master of leapfrog." Not much of an accomplishment, considering. "Fernando, please. There's not much time. We have to go. Now."

Argh. Precious time was ticking away. Mike could be awake by now. I stood and threw up my hands. Forget it. If Fernando wanted to be stubborn, there was nothing I could do about it.

I shut the bedroom door, breaking my rule of not leaving him alone again. What choice did I have?

A quick look out the blinds showed me that Lady Luck was still rooting for me. I tugged on my boots, tossed on my coat and hat and slipped out the door with a flashlight in gloved hand. So much drama that could've been avoided if only the place had a back door.

I took off, darting over to the next block, not stopping until I was sure he hadn't woken up and noticed. I'd high-five myself if there were two of me. The park was my first stop, the second would depend on what, if anything, was discovered at the first.

The fence now had police tape all over it, in addition to the tunnel itself. No doubt spurred by my previous disregard for the law. I had one foot inside a chain-link when movement caught my attention. I whipped my head around in time to catch a flash of red zipping over the bridge, passing under the streetlight, and disappearing into the darkness. I quickly pulled the flashlight from my pocket and yanked my foot out.

Oof! And landed flat on my back as a result. I patted around for the light that had flown out of my hand. Not finding it, I scrambled up and brushed off.

"Violet?" I yelled, then raced off in the direction she'd gone.

I was mystified. There was no way she could have gotten away so fast. She hadn't gained that much of a lead on me. I shouldn't have called out her name, but it'd been a knee-jerk reaction.

I continued on the footpath that circled the waterfront, praying I didn't encounter an icy patch, and smashed right into one of the piers that had been removed for the winter.

"Ow!"

Obviously, not a pier. Piers didn't talk. Although, it *was* Bigfoot Bay; anything was possible.

I staggered back, seeing stars. Dawn was approaching, and if I focused hard enough, I could make out a familiar face.

"Mrs. Fairchild?" I rushed over and grasped her. I'd just had a head-on collision with my mom's best friend, who was more than double my age, and she'd handled the accident better than me. Even her coffee hadn't spilled. "I am so sorry. Are you okay?"

"Yes, dear. A little taken off guard but no harm done. What has you scurrying around this early in the morning?"

"I saw Violet. I was trying to catch up with her."

"Violet?" Mrs. Fairchild swiveled her head around. "Where?"

"You were coming from the other direction. You didn't see her run by in her red coat?"

"I'm afraid not." Her eyes filled with concern. I thought she was going to place a hand on my forehead. "Are you feeling well, dear?"

"I... I think so." I *knew* I saw her. I thought I saw her. *Dang it.* I had no idea if I saw her or not. Maybe my suspicion about getting the wrong drink hadn't been so unrealistic. Could Skull Root induce hallucinations too?

"You've been missing her, haven't you? Wanting something badly enough can play tricks on you." I nodded, not sure what I was agreeing to. "But when she returns from her little vacation, don't you think you'll be the first one she sees?"

"I hope so." She patted my shoulder, and I eyed the Bigfoot Café to-go cup in her hand. "I didn't know they opened so early."

"Five on weekdays. Very convenient for us early birds. I always try and get a bit of fresh air and exercise before the rest of the town wakes up. A cup or two of strong coffee is the carrot I need to haul myself out of bed."

From what I could tell, a normal amount of steam rose from the hole in the lid. "It doesn't look like one of those strange smoky drinks I see everyone getting lately."

She laughed. "Good heavens, no. Call me old-school, but I don't see the allure of those things. But they do seem to be very popular."

Yes, too popular. How much simpler would life be if only one person in town drank them—namely, Clarisse—instead of everyone and their mother?

"I'll let you get back to your walk now," I said. "Sorry again for crashing into you. I need to pay better attention."

"Pfff. No worries. It was a good diversion."

"Diversion? Is there..." I paused when I noticed a man standing near the fence.

"Something wrong, dear?"

"There's a guy staring at us." The sun had risen enough to notice his scrutiny. He more resembled an odd duck than a man wearing a suit.

Mrs. Fairchild followed my gaze. "Oh, pay him no mind. It's probably just another one of those insurance investigators. There's so much hoopla going on right now, especially since the authorities have Jed Kent held for questioning."

"Who's Jed Kent?"

"The attendant who was in charge of the ice tunnel exhibit when... when you had your unfortunate discovery," she whispered as if it were a secret.

The guy who'd let us into the exhibit that night had said it'd taken a little longer than the others to set up, and Griffin and I had been the first ones to enter. "They think he had something to do with Misty's death?"

"Not directly, but there's talk that he's covering for the ice company. You know how it is around here. So much gossip. There's speculation that he was paid off to keep his mouth shut. Personally, I think it's hogwash. Our beloved festival has been around for decades, and never once was there a safety issue. Now, all of a sudden, they're making a stink?"

Mrs. Fairchild's head trembled enough to pop off; I worried for her blood pressure. I placed my hand on her arm to calm her.

"Like some melting ice killed that girl," she continued. "What a load of rubbish."

So, Griffin wasn't blowing anything out of proportion. It really was believed the area was dangerous.

"Do you know why Misty was even near the tunnel if it was closed down? This Jed Kent guy told us it wasn't ready until right before we arrived."

"Because she was scheduled. She worked for parks and rec."

Oh. That was new information. "Was Clarisse Jones also hanging around the area?" Even if it all turned out to be some freak accident, I still felt she was guilty of something.

"Clarisse? No, why?"

"I don't trust her."

She chuckled. "No one does. Fortunately, she doesn't leave her house much."

Huh. Lucky me. I'd been in town just shy of four days and saw her for half of them. "Well, thanks for chatting with me, Mrs. Fairchild. I should get back to the shop in case Violet shows up."

She squeezed my hand. "You do that. I'm sure she'll be back before you know it. Give her my love."

"Will do."

"And don't forget to stop by and visit me at the hotel before you leave town."

"I won't forget. Promise."

The man who'd been gawking at us was nowhere in sight, and I debated about returning and hopping the fence, completing my original mission.

I ended up walking away. After what Mrs. Fairchild had told me about the attendant, it'd be ill-advised on my part to continue snooping around as if consequences didn't apply to me. It was like I was morphing into my sister. She was the 'punch first, ask questions later' sibling, and I was the sensible one. But here I was, barely thinking twice before jumping off a building just because there was a conclusion at the bottom.

What I needed to do was come up with a reasonable plan. That was the only way I'd find Violet. I crossed the street, shielding my eyes from the sun with my hand. When I got back to the shop, I would—

Mike. I darted inside the nearest entrance and was greeted by a divine smell. Freshly ground coffee. Was it a coincidence that the closest store was a coffee house and not a fish factory? I didn't care in the slightest.

I peeked out the window, confident Mike hadn't seen me.

He cruised down the street, probably on his way to the park. Whew, that was close.

When I turned around, there were ten eyes on me. *What? You've never seen a grown woman act paranoid before?* I flashed a big smile and stepped up to the counter.

"Hey, I know you. Easy girl."

"Excuse me?"

"Your order, nice and easy. Plain black coffee. Dark roast."

"Oh. Okay."

"Will it be the same today?"

"Sure." I rooted around in my jacket pocket. I hadn't planned on buying anything, but at least I had the option since I'd started keeping money in my coat instead of my purse. Wouldn't want Fernando to choke on a coin.

"I never got your name." He pulled up a cup and filled it with fresh, hot heaven.

"It's… Samm." What the heck, it was easier this way. "And yours?"

"Zed."

"Nice to meet you, Zed. Again."

"Likewise."

Zed the Zen guy. Should be easy enough to remember. I handed him a few bills while glimpsing the pastry case. It was slim pickings: A couple of cinnamon scones, one oat bran muffin, and zero chocolate chip banana bread.

"Not much out today," I said. "I know Amy's been unavailable, but don't you have other bakers who supply the café?"

He shrugged. "You'd have to ask Clare. She's in the back."

I stepped to the side so Zed could give another customer a refill. I sipped my brew, waiting for the chance to talk with him further. Working in the town's most popular coffee shop, I figured he might have some insight into… Uh, what was that behind the counter? I drummed my fingers, urging him to finish up.

"Hey, Zed. Is anyone else in the back besides Clare?"

"No."

My heart throbbed harder. "Could you get her for me, please?"

"Sure."

I crossed my fingers he wouldn't just yell for her, catching a break when he left the front and went out of my sight.

Without another thought, I reached over the counter and snatched the red coat, then tore out of that café like the rest of my life depended on it.

Because it did.

CHAPTER THIRTEEN

I sprinted full throttle all the way to the shop, slamming the door behind me. Clutching the red coat, I caught my breath and tried to quiet my mind long enough to solve the puzzle.

Never mind that I'd just channeled my inner Violet, running off with the coat right after making the resolution to tone things down. None of that mattered anymore because I knew who was responsible for Misty's death.

Clare. It was Clare.

Holy moly, I'd figured it out.

One, she had access to enough dry ice to freeze a herd of elephants. Two, she had Violet's coat, which meant it was her, not my sister, who'd been on the bridge the morning of the festival.

Now, I just needed proof that she'd been in possession of chicaweed and had the knowledge to pull it all off. I should search her place too, see if she was growing any of those stupor-inducing ferns I read about…

Wait—why *did* she have Violet's coat?

I scoured it over, inspecting the tag as if expecting it to be labeled with a name like a toddler's. I had to face the possibility that it wasn't Violet's coat at all. I ran to her bedroom closet and rummaged through, looking for anything long and red. Okay, there was no coat. But that still didn't prove anything. Violet could've been wearing it the night she left. And Clare could own the exact same one. Just because Mrs. Stein said no one else paraded around in that color, didn't make it law.

Think, Samm, think. If only I could connect a few more dots, I'd be able to go to Damon. I'd also be helping Mrs. Fairchild in the process. Since her hotel sponsored the event, I couldn't imagine a scandal like this boding too well for business.

But first, before anything else, I needed to check on Fernando. He had to have gotten over his grudge by now. When I looked toward the bed, I saw him sitting on top of the locked box that I'd never shoved back to its hiding place underneath the bed. The way he looked up at me tumbled my heart around my chest. I'd been so excited, but nothing I'd discovered so far had led me any closer to Violet.

Which meant my fiancé was no closer to warm-bloodedness either.

The rap on the front door had him leaping off the box and diving under the bed. What I really wanted to do was join him. I didn't want to leave the room at all, not when it was probably just someone who wanted to lecture me. Ahem, Mike or Griffin.

After the third knock, I ventured out. It wouldn't hurt to look in case it was Sage. I peeked out and spotted Amy. Shoot. I'd forgotten about her tea.

I unlocked the door. "Amy! It's so good to see you out and about."

She stepped inside. "Thanks. I'm just wondering if you found that calming tea yet? I could really use it right now. I had a terrible night."

"Yep, I found it. I was meaning to let you know, but I got a little wrapped up in something."

"I bet you did," she mumbled.

"What?"

"Nothing." She smiled. "Ditzy me, I almost forgot." She pulled a small wrapped loaf from her coat pocket. "I made you some chocolate chip banana bread. Perfectly cooked. No charred edges."

"Oh... great. How thoughtful." I set it on the counter. "Let me grab that tea for you."

"Thanks."

"Hey, does this mean you're baking again? I was at the café earlier, and they're wiped out of almost everything."

"That's what I've been doing all morning. It feels so good to finally put all this behind me and get on with my life."

She was pretty chipper for having such a terrible night but good for her. I went into the storage closet and pulled down the jar of chamomile.

Amy was right behind me. "Not that one, silly." She pointed to the chicaweed. "That one."

"No, that's not the right stuff. That's..." Um, how did she know? It was like she knew the jars had been switched but didn't know they'd been switched back. Or... "Is there another plant whisperer in town?" I asked, chuckling.

"Plant whisperer? You crack me up, Samm."

I couldn't pinpoint why my gut felt so topsy-turvy. "It's chamomile you want, not chicaweed. I'm sure of it. I consulted with Sage."

"Interesting tidbit. Did you know chicaweed is a cousin of the banana plant? In fact, I've baked with it before and you can't even tell the difference."

I slowly turned around. Her grin was a little too Cheshire

cat-like. "Yeah, that is interesting. But I'm not sure why you're telling me."

She thrust the bread that was supposed to be sitting on the counter in my face. "Here, try for yourself."

"Uh, no thanks. I'm not really a banana person." *Thrash thrash thrash*. My little stomach flips had transformed into a tsunami, crashing my heart into my throat.

"Don't be rude. It's delicious."

"I already ate, but make sure to leave it here when you go and I'll have some later when—"

"I said try it."

Holy Shih Tzu… *is that a gun?* The barrel pointed under her coat, aimed right at me. I took a step back. "Amy, what are you doing? Calm down."

The creepiest thing was that she'd never stopped smiling. "Look, I'll even go first." With one hand she somehow peeled back the wrapper and broke off a piece, all while continuing to eyeball me. She popped it into her mouth. "Yum. Told you it's delicious." She cracked off a hunk and shoved it to my lips. "Your turn."

Was she disturbed enough to also drug herself in order to convince me to eat some? No, I decided. She already had a gun; she didn't have to do anything she didn't want to do. None of it made any sense, and I told her so.

"You're a smart girl, Samm. Or should I call you Eve?" She smirked. "I don't blame you for being hesitant about my bread. Do you have any idea what high amounts of chicaweed can do to a person? I'm sure you do. I can tell by your face. But what you might not know is that I experimented a whole lot and discovered that baking weakens the toxin, nearly rendering it inactive. So, sampling some won't hurt you in the slightest." Her smile inverted and she shot me a dagger. "Eat it."

The second the bread passed through my lips, hers lifted again as if a puppet master had yanked her strings.

"There, that wasn't so bad, was it?" As if to prove her point, she consumed another large piece.

Blech. Yeah, it really *was* that bad. It tasted like banana-flavored paste. Even the chocolate couldn't redeem it. I detached my tongue from the roof of my mouth and made a face.

She pouted. "Aww, I'm offended."

"Told you I didn't like banana," I rasped.

"Oh well." She shrugged. "More for me." She scarfed down another pasty lump. "Mmm."

Who was this woman, and what did she do with sweet little Amy? Since she'd swallowed more than triple the amount of my helping, I no longer worried about dying so much as going—in any other context, the pun might be funny—bananas.

"Misty used to love my bread. I couldn't make it fast enough." She giggled. "I used to tease her that she was turning yellow and sprouting a stem."

"You must really miss her," I said, sincerely. Since Misty had been her only family, I wondered if she'd been driven mad with grief and just wanted to see someone enjoying her banana bread again. Stranger things had been known to happen. I should know, I had the evidence croaking in the bedroom.

"Miss her? You have got to be kidding. She deserved everything she got."

"I know she wasn't the nicest person, but as you said yourself, she was family…" My throat was tight. Water… I needed water.

"Ha! Family doesn't turn on you like that." I made a move to get a bottle from the fridge, but she grabbed my arm. "Don't even think about it. Stay right here."

"I only want some water."

"Remember how I said the bread wouldn't hurt you? That is

true, but only on its own."

Warning bells were clanging away in my brain. I'd been underestimating her, making excuses for her odd behavior because this was Amy Evans. I'd known her my entire life, and she was the kindest person you could ever meet.

"Have you tried one of those special lattes from Bigfoot Café yet? If not, you're in for a treat. That's another thing Misty loves —oops!—*loved*."

"It was you," I whispered. "You killed her."

She giggled again and I wanted to throw up. That actually sounded like a good plan. Whatever chicaweed was in me via the bread needed to come out.

"She was after my man. I couldn't have that."

"Your man?"

I had to keep her talking then distract her somehow. She was a little thing; I could've taken her easily if it weren't for that blasted gun in her coat. But if I could knock it away, then—

"And now *you're* after him."

"What?"

She tsked, shaking her head. "I liked you a lot, Samm. I really did. How could you betray me like this?"

"Amy, I really don't know what you're talking about."

She let out an exaggerated sigh. "Mike. You think I didn't notice the way he looked at you at my house? He was there to check up on *me*, to make sure *I* was doing okay, but instead, he focused on *you*. Then I find him parked outside the shop all night? That was the final crushing straw."

"No, you don't understand—"

"Oh, I understand perfectly." She was beginning to resemble a rabid dog, and since my nervous system was firing off like gangbusters, it must've been contagious. "And you can't take him from me. I simply won't allow it."

"I have a fiancé. I don't want Mike. Please, believe me."

"Now, that's rich." She laughed. More like cackled. "You know what? Everyone thought of Misty as the bad one, but you two are more alike than you realize." I was thinking the exact same thing about her. "Would you betray your own sister too?"

Violet. The nausea intensified, and I covered my mouth. No, this was a good thing. I needed to get it out, but I worried that all the fear coursing through me would make me pass out first.

"Just a friendly public service announcement," she said, all peaches and cream. "If you puke, you'll be eating it up, since you already declined more of my delicious bread. I bet you're kicking yourself for that now."

"What have you done with Violet?"

The entire time I'd suspected that my sister had had a hand in Misty's death because of what she'd done to Fernando, but the possibility that Violet might be another one of Amy's victims just became very real.

"I didn't do anything to Violet. She's one of my favorite people." She appeared genuinely distressed over the question.

"Then where is she?"

"How should I know? But what I do know is that you should be thanking me right now. I did you a favor."

"A *favor*?" This woman not only switched personalities quicker than a psychologist's dream case study, but she also had more bats in her noodle than a vampire's macaroni art project.

"Misty was going to do away with Violet during the grand reopening of the ice festival. Had it all planned out and everything. And I stopped her." Amy lifted her chin like she was proud of herself. "I used her own spell against her. She never saw it coming. If it weren't for me, your sister would be dead right now instead of mine."

My head was in a wind tunnel. "What do you mean by 'spell'?" There was so much getting thrown at me, I couldn't possibly dodge it all.

"Misty had worked on it all week. Poor thing. It made her so weak. I guess she still wasn't as powerful as she thought." She narrowed her eyes at me. "Not everyone is so lucky."

I needed to sit down, but I didn't dare lower myself to a more vulnerable position. "Worked on what all week, exactly?"

"The freezing spell for Violet. Misty hated her, you know. Your sister got in her way all the time, so she finally decided to do something about it. The potion she created and planted in Violet's iced tea was supposed to freeze her lungs, but I couldn't let that happen. Unfortunately for Misty, she'd just eaten my herbal banana bread. The chicaweed was circulating through her system just like it's currently doing in yours."

From what I'd read in the library, I understood the connection between high doses of the herb and carbon dioxide, but how did a spell fit into all of this? Misty wasn't a witch.

"I'm not drinking one of those stupid smoking lattes." As far as I knew, she didn't have one stowed away alongside her gun. Did she think she was going to drag me into a public coffee shop and demand I buy one?

"Weren't you listening before? You've offended me again, and I'm starting to take it personally." She chomped on more bread, turning my mouth sour. "I said baking—which means heat to you non-bakers—inactivates the poison. But did you know it can be reactivated? And did you also know that those special smoky lattes can be cold-brewed, as well? They don't advertise that fact because they're even more difficult to make, but you can ask for them." She shook her head. "Poor Misty. Too bad she didn't know all that either. She didn't know that my secret weapon was ticking away inside her stomach while she hid in the tunnel, while she waited to trigger the spell at the exact right moment before Violet was due to show. If only she'd known about the chicaweed, she would've known all that was needed to finish the job was a special iced drink. A special iced drink I made sure we picked up from the café before arriving at the festival."

"So, this really had nothing to do with a spell." Misty could've been delusional, when in the end, it'd all boiled down to science. "What about that one rainforest fern you have to mix with the chicaweed—where'd you get that from?" *Please don't say Violet's shop.*

"I'm not sure if you're that daft or that arrogant."

"You left out baffled as one of the options."

"I have no idea about this fern you're babbling about but of course it had to do with a spell." Amy rolled her eyes, apparently at my stupidity. "Misty was so wiped out from casting it that she became dizzy and had to sit down, and my being the helpful, loving sister that I am made sure she drank plenty of liquid, in the form of coffee, of course. Although…" She tapped her lips. "I have to admit it worked out much better than I expected. I only planned to anesthetize her enough to force the spelled tea into her, ending her the same way she'd intended to do to Violet, but the combination of all three forces intensified each other. It didn't just freeze her lungs; it froze her entire body into the tunnel wall."

Holy crud. Talk about psychotic. "That, uh, sounds like a lot of work." Amy made it sound like she was boasting about it, like she deserved a prize for her accomplishment. Maybe I could use that to my advantage.

"Well, I couldn't exactly be scatterbrained about it, that's for sure. I kept my head together and reaped the rewards. My sister is no longer a problem, yours is alive and well, and Bay Ice Sculpture is going to be held responsible. After Misty froze, I slipped out the exit with the evidence, went home and destroyed it, and no one's the wiser."

Except me. "Why are you telling me all your secrets?" Although, I already knew why, and it made me shudder. I was aware of what she wanted to do to me, but I didn't know how she was going to do it. I had to buy time.

"Because, despite you double-crossing me, I feel a kinship with you. Enough to want you to be aware of exactly how you're going to die. You should feel honored. I didn't even extend that same courtesy to my own blood."

"Honored?" I gurgled out a laugh.

"I didn't destroy *all* the evidence. I saved some of the spelled iced tea, and now I think it's time to take a little walk to the park. Nice day for it too. The sun is shining. Spring is coming. You can feel it in the air. The sculptures aren't safe right now. If someone is foolish enough to go inside one, they could suffer the same fate as my poor sister."

"I'm not going with you."

Her coat rose higher, and I stepped back. "It appears my friend disagrees with you."

A crash against the front door startled us both, and I took that opportunity to slam into her. She stumbled back, and before she regained her bearings, the door burst open. Damon and Griffin.

"Be careful," I yelled. "She's got a—"

A curved, yellow object plopped from her coat onto the ground.

A banana?

"You have got to be kidding me!" I screeched, all the built-up tension racing to get out of me. "A freaking *banana*?!"

Griffin put his arms around me. "It's okay, Sammi. You can relax now."

"I can't believe you did this to me!" I shouted over his shoulder. "You know where you can shove all your precious bananas."

Damon was hauling Amy off as she yelled back at me, "All that work for nothing! You don't know what it's like, you don't know how hard it is—you're magical everywhere, and you don't even care. We need to use the town's energy, and it's still not easy!"

"Quiet," Damon hissed.

The last thing I heard when Damon dragged her out the door was, "Hey, is Mike with you?"

"Wait!" I tried to shimmy out of Griffin's hold. "I have stuff to tell him. Important stuff. There's so much he needs to know. Amy killed Misty." I yanked harder. Why wasn't he letting me go?

"Calm down. He already knows."

"He does?" I stilled. "How?"

"We were able to get everything from your call. Quick thinking, by the way, hitting the speaker. As soon as we figured out what was going on, Damon was able to reach the station and get it on record."

"My call? What are you talking about?"

"What are *you* talking about? You called me right after Amy arrived. Fortunately, Damon was over and we were both able to hear it."

"Griffin, I didn't call you."

"Well, someone did."

My dead haunted cell phone sitting on the corner table rang once, startling the bejeebers out of me.

I jumped from his arms, and this time he released me. There was absolutely no reason why he should've been holding me for that long, and we both knew it.

He cleared his throat. "I guess that's it, then." I nodded, still staring at my phone. "I'm glad you're okay, Samm."

"Me too. Someone must be watching out for me."

Ring.

Translation: *You're welcome.*

EPILOGUE

"*I* guess this means you're going back to Chicago soon."

I was curled up on the couch in a blanket, sipping the strong, hot coffee that Griffin had been kind enough to bring me that morning. Fernando was frolicking in the bathtub.

"You'd think."

That was what someone with a normal life would do, but I didn't have a normal life. Not anymore. I was no longer on town arrest, but I wouldn't be going anywhere until I had my man back.

"You're not? Why?"

"It's complicated." I really hated when people gave that type of canned response, but in this case, it was the best choice of words.

"What about your fiancé?"

"I still have one, if that's what you're asking. And I'm warning you—don't even think about bad-mouthing him."

Wow. That'd come out way snippier than intended, but in my defense, it'd been less than twenty-four hours since the whole

Amy fiasco, and I was tired and cranky. In retrospect, I hadn't been in much danger, but I didn't know that at the time. I hadn't a clue she was packing fruit instead of heat.

He put his hands up. "Don't shoot. I come in peace."

I sighed. "I'm sorry. I didn't mean to snap. It was really nice of you to take time out of your day to fuel me with caffeine. Thank you."

"You're welcome, and you're forgiven."

"Especially because you're probably swamped with work. I bet you're in the middle of a really great scene, and I'm preventing you from finishing."

"Nah, it's all right. I'm flexible. I'll get my writing in later."

"What did you say your pseudonym was again?"

His lips curved up. "I didn't."

I drummed my fingers on my knee. "So… you were engaged, huh?" His eyebrows rose, and I shrugged. "Sage may have mentioned it."

"Are you asking me a question you already know the answer to, or is there more to it?"

Okay, this was crazy, and so was Sage and her theories. The things she came up with. Why would it bother me if Griffin moved on without me? I'd expect it. I'd insist upon it. When I left town all those years before, I had no intention of ever coming back. If I wanted him to spend the rest of his life alone, that'd be just plain cruel.

"Yes and no. Never mind."

"Does it bother you?"

If it did, it'd be because I wanted him to be happy, and according to Sage, the woman was an evil shrieking harpy who ate puppies for breakfast. Or maybe that'd been my interpretation. But she did say his ex-fiancée was no one I'd care to know, and I trusted her opinion. Unless that opinion extended to how much said engagement upset me.

"Why would it bother me? That'd be silly. Especially since I'm engaged right now."

"I'm well aware."

I gnawed on my lip a while before blurting out, "What happened between the two of you?" Since we were on the subject, I was going to combust if I didn't at least ask why they were no longer together.

"I'd tell you but it's too complicated."

His smirk told me I'd deserved that. I was mulling over an equally smart-alecky response when there was a bang at the door.

"That's probably Sage," I said. "When I talked to her last night, she said she was stopping by today." I pulled back the shades and checked out the window. Definitely not Sage. "It's your brother. Any idea why he's here again?" I liked to be prepared.

"Nope."

Officer Damon had already paid me a visit once Amy was safely locked away in a cell—or wherever they put a person who'd just confessed to murder. Along with more of his police-y questions, I'd also learned the rest of the scoop. It turned out Jed the attendant *was* keeping a secret, but not for Bay Ice Sculptures, Inc. It was for Misty. She'd blackmailed him into closing off the tunnel exhibit for a couple of hours or else she threatened to tell his wife about the little affair they had. But once he'd heard Amy's confession, he broke down and spilled everything.

Damon and I had no more ground to cover, unless he was there to speak to me about Violet. Again. He'd noticed the red coat I'd taken from the coffee house, and of course, recognized it immediately. I hadn't meant to get his hopes up like that, but I had to explain why it was in her shop without Violet inside it.

And surprisingly through it all, never once had Damon or

Griffin ever questioned Amy's mention of spells or magic. I chalked it off to them thinking it was the ramblings of a hysterical killer who'd ingested too much chicaweed.

"He's not going to leave until you let him in."

"Right." I opened the door and smiled. "Damon. What brings you by this fine morning?"

"Samm." He nodded and came inside, pausing when he spotted Griffin. He glanced back and forth between us. "Am I disturbing anything?"

Griffin held up his cup. "Just swung by to bring Samm some coffee."

"How considerate."

There was an unspoken conversation going on between the two brothers, and I didn't like it. I cleared my throat. "What's up, Officer?"

Damon turned back to me. "I just came from having a little chat with Clare. She swears Violet gave her the coat."

"Why would she do that?"

"I don't know. Clare said she likes to… collect things, and she earned it fair and square."

"What's that supposed to mean? I'm not giving her back the coat. I don't believe her."

"She has some quirks, but I have no reason not to give her the benefit of the doubt."

"Then you do that, but I'm not."

"It's not as if we have Violet here to confirm or deny. Speaking of…"

I shook my head. "No, I haven't heard anything since you last asked me eight hours ago. I guess she's still avoiding me, but I can't imagine it'll be for much longer. She has a shop to run."

I said the same words I'd been saying on repeat, explaining to everyone why Violet wasn't around, but they were starting to lose credibility in my head. The pit in my stomach was growing larger, and I was trying my hardest not to read anything into it, but the more I tried to reason with my brain, the more my gut suffered.

"It's been five days. That must've been some fight."

"Believe me, it was." He looked like he was about to fire off more questions I didn't want to answer, so I redirected. "What about Clarisse Jones?"

"What about her?"

"Did you follow up on what I told you?"

"That you believe she was lying about being sick? That's not a crime, Samm."

"It is if she was doing something illegal in the process. And stealing's a crime, is it not?"

"Once again, do you have any proof she actually stole herbs from Violet?"

I crossed my arms. "No." I wanted to play her at her own game but didn't want to sink to her level of scumminess. I had no clue if the feverfew jar had been empty before she'd arrived. "I don't trust her, Damon. Just because I don't have evidence, doesn't mean she isn't doing something wrong."

"Most of the town don't trust her. Get used to it. She's an outsider who married an obscenely rich elderly man who'd give up his right kidney to the first person who asked. Some may question her morals, but she's not a criminal."

Hmph.

Damon left shortly afterward, and I felt a flush of satisfaction seeing Violet's coat remain in the shop. He'd never made me hand it over. That was cool of him.

Even if he hadn't taken me seriously about Conniving Clarisse.

"Things have been pretty surreal for you since you've been back, huh?"

"You don't know the half of it."

I barely knew, and I was living it. Misty's murder had been solved, and I still wasn't one step closer to finding Violet. After what she did to Fernando, I should've been building the spit I planned to roast her on, but tinges of worry kept slipping in and ruining my plans. Amy claimed that Misty had devised a spell against my sister, and I was going bonkers wondering if it was true.

A *spell*. But how was that possible? Misty wasn't a witch.

"Just promise me one thing, Sammi."

"What's that?" I glanced up from the blanket I was twisting into knots. His expression was solemn.

"You won't leave this time without saying goodbye."

Oh, Griff. I wanted so badly to grant him that promise, but I just couldn't. What if something happened outside my control and I had to break it? That would be worse. I already felt two inches tall, and I knew that hadn't been his intention. Griffin was too good of a person to do that to me.

He leaned toward me, and my heart went nuts. He reached his hand over, and I scooted back a bit, thinking he was going to brush the hair from my face. That would've been more intimate than I was comfortable with.

"What are you doing?" I whispered.

"You have a little something behind your ear."

"Seriously, Griffin. What are you—twelve?" Had I misread the moment or what? "You're doing the quarter thing again?"

He swiped his hand over the side of my head, barely touching me. "Nope, not a quarter. It's… it's… what the heck is this thing anyway?" He held up something red, flopping it back and forth.

I flattened my lips, peering closer. Then I busted out laughing.

"Nothing like a gummy lobster to lighten the mood," he said, biting off the head.

I couldn't even begin to fathom where he'd been hiding that thing, but I was grateful for the diversion. He was giving me an out instead of pressing me to make a promise I couldn't keep.

He tossed the gummy at me. "The tail's yours if you want it."

In between fits of residual laughter, I said, "You're not worried about me getting sick?"

Way back when we were only in the single digits, we used to wolf down bags of those things. One day on the playground, Callie Nelson bet me her unicorn hat that I couldn't eat a monster bag of jumbo gummy lobsters in under a minute. Since Violet had just turned my unicorn hat into a praying mantis the night before, I couldn't resist the challenge. Griffin and Sage cheered me on the entire time until there was just one gummy left. I turned around, and he could see it in my face—one more and I'd be toast. He told me not to do it, but I didn't listen. I swallowed that last one, then proceeded to spew out large quantities of corn syrup and Red No. 40 all over my shoes. Ah, good times.

"Well, sure, if I had a whole nest of them and—" A loud clang reverberated from Violet's room. "What was that?"

I groaned. What now? "I'll go check. Hold on."

He put his arm out. "You stay here. I'll look."

"No, I got it. Really." He ignored me, bolting toward the bedroom. Argh. "There's nothing to worry about anymore, remember? No melting ice sculptures in there."

No comment. I was right on his heels when he opened the door. While he scanned the room, I darted past and inched open the bathroom door, searching for Fernando. No sign of him but the culprit lay on the tile floor—a chrome towel rack. Now, how in the world had he knocked *that* off the wall? In my peripheral, I saw his chameleon skin blending in with the woodwork. In another blink, he was gone, just when Griffin came up behind me.

"Samm! I told you to stay back." He bent down and picked up the rack. "At least we know what the noise was."

"Yeah." My eyes swept over every available surface, hoping he'd gone underneath the bed because I couldn't detect him anywhere. I did not want Griffin to see my fiancé in frog form, especially because he'd assume he was a pet. I was trying to preserve what little dignity Fernando had left.

"Let me see if I can reattach it for you. If not, I'll come back with my tools."

"Thanks."

Through the open bedroom door, I caught a glimpse of Griffin's to-go cup just before it toppled over, lid popping off and coffee spilling all over the floor. I dropped my head in my hands.

When I looked back up, I swore I saw Fernando grin before leaping away.

"Hey, is this a blueberry in the sink?"

The absurdity of the situation hit me dead-on, and laughing was a much better option than crying.

Welcome back to Bigfoot Bay, Samm.

You're not in Chicago anymore.

TROUBLE'S A-BREWING in Bigfoot Bay.

When the tavern fool is found floating in a vat of green beer at the local Irish pub, Samm can't help but get charmed into the case…

. . .

Don't miss Bewitched Brew - the next misadventure in the Bigfoot Bay Witches cozy mystery series!

Flip the page to check out the first chapter...

BEWITCHED BREW
CHAPTER ONE

Blueberries coated the inside of my purse. A wicked stained mess. I'd given up all hope of ever claiming it again for my own. It belonged to Fernando now.

I sighed then stated an apology to my fiancé-turned-frog. My sister had spelled him into another species, and here I was complaining about a bag? My priorities needed an adjustment.

"Are you talking to your purse again?"

I glanced up to my lifelong best friend, Sage, staring at me. "No." I took a sip of coffee and brought my Fernando carrier closer to my body. "Thanks for the blueberries, by the way. You have no idea how important they are to me."

"Don't you mean to your frog?"

"To us both."

Sage knew I was taking care of a frog, but she hadn't a clue that frog was also the man I planned to marry. There was no good time to have *that* conversation. For whatever reason unbeknownst to me, my carnivorous husband-to-be would only eat blueberries. But not just any blueberries. Store-bought wouldn't do for my berry snob. No, they had to be the organic ones Sage grew in her greenhouse. She fueled him with a steady supply, and we owed his life to her.

"I'm beginning to think you don't even have a pet."

I cringed at the word "pet," and I imagined Fernando did as well. For a macho guy like him, that wouldn't go over too well. I couldn't risk leaving him behind when I went out, but until they made little earmuffs, I had to do my best to shield him from unpleasant conversation. I still didn't have a handle on how much he could understand in that body.

"Then what would I be doing with all these blueberries?" I asked, and she shrugged. "I'll let you meet him soon, okay? I promise. It's just a little hard to explain right now."

"Hmph."

"Can I get you another Irish cream latte?"

I flinched at the voice. Geez, Clare. Way to sneak up on someone. "No, I'm good. Thanks."

She thrust a plateful of shamrock cookies in my face. "More cookies? On the house."

I gestured to the uneaten ones on the table. The pastry case was full again, unlike the beginning of the week, and I suspected Clare was the baker stocking it. "I haven't even finished these."

"Okay, then. Give me a holler if you need anything."

I nodded, and she returned behind the counter. It was a gloomy Friday afternoon, and Sage and I were hanging out at Bigfoot Café during one of her study breaks. I didn't know why she was even bothering to get an official plant science degree. She was already the Plant Whisperer.

"Wow, she's really laying it on thick," I said.

Sage waved her hand. "Don't be so cynical. She's just trying to be nice."

"She stole Violet's coat, and she knows she's guilty. That's why she's acting this way."

"There's no proof she stole anything. And you don't know

her like I do. She may like to collect unusual things, but that doesn't make her a thief."

"So I'm told." Officer Damon had basically said the same thing, but I didn't buy it. It was too suspicious. Who collected red coats? She was up to something even if I didn't know what that something was.

"The more important issue here is Violet. She's been gone a long time, Samm."

"Yeah." I'd been back in Bigfoot Bay for a week and a day, and my reckless witch of a sister was still hiding from me. "She also knows she's guilty."

"Aren't you starting to get even the least bit worried? What if something bad happened?"

Oh, something bad happened, all right, but it wasn't *to* her. It was *because* of her. Despite that, I couldn't prevent the fleeting thoughts from infiltrating my head several times a day, telling me something was off. My sister's shop, Violet's Soap & Tea Emporium, was her baby, and I never thought she'd abandon it for this long.

So yes, I was a teensy bit worried, but buckets more for Fernando. Without Violet, he didn't stand a chance. She was the one who cast the spell, and she was the only one who could reverse it.

"It was a *really* horrible fight, Sage."

"One that you won't give me any details to." I couldn't deny it because she was absolutely right. I was born into a family of witches, and that was not a fact you shared with others, even your best friend. Not if you wanted to keep them as one. "You have to realize Damon isn't going to accept that answer for much longer. Pretty soon, he's going to take matters into his own hands."

"I'm not stopping him from doing that now."

Since Misty's death had been solved, and I no longer

suspected my sister as the one who'd turned her into a human popsicle, the desperate urge to find her before the police department did had disappeared. Officer Damon Kane, aka Violet's lovestruck puppy, could use every ounce of his resources to search for her, but if she didn't want to be found, it wouldn't happen.

Sage leaned in and glared at me. "You can't fool me, Samm. Violet's temporary leave of absence, or whatever you want to call it, is bothering you more than you're letting on."

"It's Eve, remember?" I said, changing the subject. Eve was my middle name and the one I'd adopted after moving to Chicago thirteen years earlier. Only people from my hometown of Bigfoot Bay still called me Samm, short for Sammara.

"Yes, I remember, *Samm.*"

So much for the last-ditch effort. Even I had begun to resign myself to the old name, at least until I left town again. It was just easier this way.

"All right, you win. But give me a little more time, okay? Since I've come back, my life's been so discombobulated. I'm still adjusting."

The nice, happy, normal world I'd created for myself over the past decade had broken down in a matter of days.

As if to prove my point, the cell phone in my coat pocket rang. The one that couldn't keep a charge and was perpetually dead. Unless it was some off-the-wall caller. Or my mother. Much like Fernando, I now kept it with me wherever I went.

I swore the phone was haunted, ever since it'd been zapped through the line during Violet's spell. But even though I couldn't dial out or use it in any way except for when it charged up enough to allow an oddball call to come through, I had a soft spot for it.

After all, it'd single-handedly helped to put a killer behind bars. How many other cell phones could list that on their resume?

"Ooh! Can I answer it?"

"Let me check to see if it's my mom first." It was a game to her. Sage knew my phone was wonky but didn't know why, and whenever it rang, she begged to be the first to see who was on the other end.

I handed it over after checking the screen. She clapped then grabbed it.

"Hello?" she sang. "Hold on a sec. Hey, Samm. Do you want to donate to the Gnome Coalition?"

"The what?"

"Can you give me more information, please?" Sage said into the line. "Uh-huh... Okay... All right, got it." She held the phone to her chest. "The movement was started by a group of leprechauns with the goal of fostering deeper relations and creating unity within the elemental kingdom. If you give fifty or more, you'll get a complimentary gold brooch. Hundred or more earns you a place of honor in their wee bulletin."

"*What?*"

"We're going to have to get back to you. Thanks." She set my cell down. "It's a worthy cause. You really should consider supporting them. Leprechauns are people too."

"Uh, no they're not. They're... leprechauns." And since they didn't even exist, the entire conversation was pointless anyway.

"I meant they were people in the context of having the same rights." She shook her head. "Wow, Chicago really did a number on you."

"If you say so." Did I mention my life was bizarre? I pointed toward McGuinness Inn, the Irish pub directly across the street. "I bet it was someone in there playing a joke. You know, in the spirit of St. Patrick's Day."

"That's not till tomorrow."

"Tell that to the crowds wearing top hats and drinking green beer. They seem to be celebrating early."

She glanced over her shoulder. "That's what happens when it falls on a weekend." She raised her cup. "I'll stick to my green tea."

I toasted her with my festive latte. "I'm just glad they changed the café special early. I never want to see one of those smoky drinks again." I pushed the plate of cookies toward her. "You should have one." I offered even though I'd never seen her eat a cookie in my life. It fascinated me.

"No, thanks. You know that's not my thing."

Sage had the most peculiar tastes. She adored sweets but only in liquid form. Otherwise, I only saw her drink tea and the occasional green coffee. The only foods she consumed were vegetables and low-sugar fruit. She was wispy as a reed and glowing with health, so I guess those ten sodas a day zoomed right through her with no ill effects.

"Speaking of green things," I said. "Do you know what kind of plant looks and feels like grass?"

"Um, could it be… grass?"

"You're the plant expert here. I found it scattered all over the floor in Violet's shop the first day I arrived and it resembled fresh grass, but I really don't think it was."

"I'm not sure. If it's an exotic, that'd be Violet's area of expertise, not mine."

Right. My best friend had a knack for communicating with plants, but only the local ones. I wanted to believe she was just really good at her studies, but there were too many things I'd witnessed that couldn't be explained. I blamed the town. It had the ability to throw anyone off their rocker.

I took a sip of coffee, almost spitting it back out when I saw who'd walked through the door. She immediately zeroed in on me then stalked over. I dropped my head. Great.

"What's the matter?" Sage asked.

Clarisse I mouthed.

Sage swung around. "Clarisse! How humbled are we to be graced by your presence this fine afternoon." She bowed in her chair. "To what do we owe the honor?"

Clarisse ignored her. "Eve, how lovely to see you again. I heard you stopped by and checked up on me while I was ill. How kind of you."

Sage raised an eyebrow. Yet another thing I hadn't told her about.

"Yes, well…" I had no idea what to say. "I… heard you were drinking a lot of those smoky lattes and they weren't agreeing with you." What the heck? I couldn't have come up with something better than that?

Clarisse waved her hand. "Pish-posh. Don't listen to my house manager. She worries way too much." House manager? How *pish-posh*. Sage had her hand over her mouth, giggling. "But I am a little confused why you'd ask to see Violet."

I looked away from Sage as she shot me a laser glare. "My mistake," I told Clarisse as casually as possible. "I thought I heard something about her staying there."

Clarisse's wide eyes did not appear faked, unlike many of her past expressions. Unfortunately. It would've made things much easier if I knew where my sister was hiding out.

The woman leaned over, resting a red dragon-nailed hand on the table. Any closer and she'd spear through my cup. "Us kind need to stick together," she said quietly.

"Us kind?" What in Merlin's beard did *that* mean?

She nodded. "Especially in light of the current circumstances. Wasn't the whole debacle surrounding Misty's demise quite the shock?"

I was still stuck on "us kind." Sage must've read my mind. "Pardon my ignorance, your royal highness, but how are you and Samm even remotely similar?"

"We live in the same town, do we not? That alone promotes a strong bond, a certain loyalty to each other." She spoke directly to me as if I were the one to ask the question.

"You're not part of this town." Sage snorted.

"And I'm only visiting," I added.

Clarisse rubbed her temples. "Oh dear, I do believe I'm coming down with another migraine. I really should run along." She inched closer and whispered in my ear. "We can accomplish great things together, Eve."

She slunk off, and I briskly rubbed the heebie-jeebies off of me. "Okay, that was just plain creepy. Don't ever call me Eve again." After continually asking others to refer to me by my middle name, and repeatedly getting ignored, it disturbed me that Clarisse was the only one who paid attention.

"Wouldn't dream of it." She looked at me as if I had a lazy third eye.

"What?" I rubbed my forehead. "Do I have something on my face?"

"You're seriously asking me that? Why don't you tell me what in the heliotrope just happened?"

"Heliotrope? Is that a plant term? Because if it is—"

Sage threw up her hands. "What is freaking wrong with you?' You went to her *house*?"

"Long story."

"Are you insane?"

"Depends who you ask."

"What were you even thinking? She's a scheming shrew. You're lucky you got out in one piece."

"I had Griffin with me."

Her lips took a sharp turn upward. "I see."

"What? No, you don't." Leave it to her to make something into this. "He just... oh, never mind."

"Uh-huh. So, what's the deal with asking about Violet staying there? She'd never associate with her socially."

I finished off the rest of my latte but tried to disguise my last swallow lest Clare run over with another. I didn't want anything I hadn't seen her make. How did I know her little nice routine wasn't just an act? She was probably silently fuming about the coat and was waiting for an opportunity to get me back. I wasn't claiming she'd poison my drink, but I wouldn't put it past her to "accidentally" leave her mouth open while preparing it.

"I didn't know where my head was at, Sage. There's been a lot going on."

"Aww, you really do want to make amends with your sister. I knew it. She's important enough for you to explore every possible avenue, no matter how crazy."

"Yeah, something like that."

My phone rang again. Sage bounced in her seat, but I lifted a finger to tell her to hold on. I checked the screen.

"Sorry." I braced myself then hit Accept. "Hi, Mom."

"Don't you 'Hi, Mom' me."

"Bye, Mom?"

"Sammara Eve Hain!" Oh boy. It was going to be one of those conversations. "I cannot believe I had to hear the news from Mary. My own daughter didn't even have the decency to tell me."

"You're not exactly the easiest to reach. And besides, the last thing I wanted was to upset you even more, being so far away and all."

"Mary reached me just fine."

"You're stuck in a rainforest. Why would I trouble you over something you can't do anything about?"

"Your father's working on getting us home, I told you that. I can't help all the toucan issues on the runway, but I should be able to count on my firstborn to keep me apprised of the goings-on. Why didn't you tell me about Misty Evans?" I opened my mouth to repeat what I'd just said but didn't get the chance. "No, forget about that. Why in the blazes didn't you tell me about your scuffle at the shop? It's bad enough I worry about Violet, but now I have to worry about you too?"

"That's exactly why I didn't mention anything. I didn't want you to worry."

"That is not a good answer."

I sighed. "I'm sorry."

"How did she even get through the wards? If one enters with even a speck of malicious intent, the mugwort will stop them."

Shoot, the mugwort. My mom would crucify me if she knew I'd removed it. Violet had hung the bitter, leafy herb in the doorway of her shop, and I had gotten sick of tasting a mouthful whenever I walked in. I glanced at Sage sipping her tea. Her eyes were everywhere else, but I knew she was hanging on my every word. "I'm not sure... maybe the stuff expires?"

"Samm! Do not even tell me you dismantled the wards."

"Okay, I won't."

"I swear, your sister is three years younger but ages older in common sense."

Right. Ask any person not related to me if it was common sense to use herbs instead of a security system, and they'd look at you like you were one scale short of a mermaid tail. I'd roll my eyes if my mom wouldn't sense it in a second.

"Well, everything's fine now so it all worked out."

The so-called scuffle only happened four days ago, but it'd probably already been printed up in the Bigfoot Bay historical records. I'd barely spoken to my mom's best friend, Mary Fairchild, since the morning I'd literally run into her at the lakefront, but it would've been naïve to think she wasn't privy to every detail as if she'd lived through the experience herself. I had to constantly remind myself this wasn't Chicago.

"Is your sister home safe and sound?"

"No."

"Then everything is not fine."

While I had her on the line, I did have some questions that'd been bugging me. Sage was still pretending not to eavesdrop, so I couldn't do it here.

"It's really noisy in here," I said to both of them. "I'm gonna step outside."

"Where are you?" Mom asked.

I headed toward the door. "Coffee shop."

"Coffee? Samm, what is wrong with you?"

"They sell more than coffee at a coffee shop."

She didn't buy it, and I hadn't expected her to. "That is the absolute last thing you should be drinking. You know how intoxicating the coffee bean is and how it affects our family." I opened the door to a blast of frigid air. If all she was going to do was lecture me, I could stay inside and at least be warm. "Why do you think Violet only drinks tea? Because she's in tune with her roots, that's why."

I huddled into the corner of the brick building and dropped my head, partly to shield my face from the cold and partly because it just tended to fall on its own whenever my mom scolded me like I was an insolent teenager.

I'd discovered the joys of coffee after I left town at thirteen. I was never allowed so much as a sip in Bigfoot Bay, but once I found out how much it helped to normalize me, not to mention how delicious it was, I died and went to java heaven. Maybe avoiding the potent brew would connect me more to my witchy side, but that was the best reason to drink it. Also, because it tasted ah-mazing.

She tsked then continued, "And on top of all the stress you've undergone? I'm surprised you didn't pass out for a week. You're lucky you're not lying facedown in a dirty alley right now."

"You know there're no dirty alleys in Bigfoot Bay. They're probably curtained and carpeted and..." I'd just remembered something. If one of us in the family mixed a large dose of coffee with an adrenaline surge, it'd knock us out like a clean uppercut to the jaw. Our chemical makeup wouldn't tolerate the combination. Since my previous life had been relatively stress-free in comparison to this past week, I wouldn't have experienced that reaction before.

That was why I'd fallen asleep after drinking the triple espresso from Sage. She hadn't inadvertently switched Mike's cup with mine, after all. How had I completely forgotten about that wacky side effect?

But now that I had remembered, did it mean I was switching to tea? Ha. Not a chance. I just had to be more conscious of my stress levels. Not an easy feat when your fiancé croaked out his sweet nothings.

"Are you sassing me?"

"Sorry, Mom." I raised my head when I heard a ruckus coming from the pub. Either the drunken customers were brawling or having a fantastic time. I couldn't tell which. "I am curious about something, though. A comment was made about Misty casting a spell, but she's not a witch. Also, something about needing to use the town's energy to perform magic. Do you have any idea what that's about?"

"Of course. Bigfoot Bay is a powerful place. Everyone knows that. *You* should know that. It was part of your studies growing up."

"Is that why our family has magic?"

She sighed this time. "No, dear, we're witches. I know you'd prefer otherwise, but really, Samm. Pay attention. You could use your skills in Chicago if you wanted to. You could use them on the moon. You'd know that if—"

"But what about Misty?" I blurted out. Geez. She didn't have to use every opportunity to tell me how I'd neglected to follow my path.

A glass filled with what I assumed to be green beer flew out the pub door, shattering and splattering on the ground. There was a bunch of shouting, but I couldn't make out anything except for a few choice obscenities.

"One can cast spells without being a witch."

What? That didn't make sense. As far as I was concerned, witch and spell were synonymous. Static burst through the line, alerting me the call would disconnect soon.

"What does that even mean?" I asked.

I winced when a man tumbled out next, bouncing face-first down the pub's concrete stairs. Ouch. That had to hurt. Since he appeared quite a bit older than your typical college-aged drinker, I was about to rush over when he picked up his head and looked around.

"Mary's expecting a visit from you soon," Mom said, ignoring my question. "You'd better not wait too long to get over to the hotel and see her."

The call dropped before I could reply.

The very drunk—or very clumsy—man stood and brushed himself off like his nosedive hadn't fazed him in the least. The pub door swung open, and he glanced back and yelled, "It wasn't me! I didn't do it!"

Then he took off down the street as if a pack of hellhounds was nipping at his heels.

Thanks for reading!

I hope you enjoyed the first book in the series as much I loved writing it. I have so much more planned for Samm and the rest of the motley crew, so if you like magic, mystery, and merry mayhem, make sure to check out the rest of the Bigfoot Bay Witches series!

Also, feel free to sign up for my list if you want to stay updated on new releases and sales. There'll also be the occasional exclusive short story that only members of the group will receive. See you there!

Bewitchingly yours,

Cat

ABOUT THE AUTHOR

Cat Larson never has to look further than her own backyard for inspiration - her small, eccentric Midwestern town with its own cast of colorful characters provides plenty of fuel for her imagination.

She's surrounded by acres of untamed forest and lakes with no shortage of peculiar creatures to write about. While sipping her first of many cups of coffee for the day and popping handfuls of wild blueberries, Cat is greeted by the extended family of frogs who share her land.

However, unlike her stories, none of these frogs were once human (that she's aware of).

THE BIGFOOT BAY WITCHES SERIES

9 781736 562604